To Marry Her Marquess

Heart of a Duke

USA TODAY BESTSELLER
CHRISTI CALDWELL

To Marry Her Marquess
Heart of a Duke Series

Copyright © 2022 by Christi Caldwell

All rights reserved. No part of this book may be reproduced in any form by any electronic or mechanical means—except in the case of brief quotations embodied in critical articles or reviews—without written permission.

The characters and events portrayed in this book are fictitious. Any similarity to real persons, living or dead, is purely coincidental and not intended by the author.

This Book is licensed for your personal enjoyment only. This Book may not be re-sold or given away to other people. If you would like to share this book with another person, please purchase an additional copy for each recipient. If you're reading this book and did not purchase it or borrow it, or it was not purchased for your use only, then please return it and purchase your own copy. Thank you for respecting the hard work of the author.

For more information about the author:
www.christicaldwellauthor.com
christicaldwellauthor@gmail.com
Twitter: @ChristiCaldwell
Or on Facebook at: Christi Caldwell Author

For first glimpse at covers, excerpts, and free bonus material, be sure to sign up for my monthly newsletter!

Printed in the USA.

Cover Design and Interior Format
© THE KILLION GROUP INC.

OTHER TITLES BY CHRISTI CALDWELL

ALL THE DUKE'S SINS
Along Came a Lady
Desperately Seeking a Duchess

ALL THE DUKE'S SIN'S PREQUEL SERIES
It Had to Be the Duke
One for My Baron

SCANDALOUS AFFAIRS
A Groom of Her Own
Taming of the Beast
My Fair Marchioness
It Happened One Winter

HEART OF A DUKE
In Need of a Duke—Prequel Novella
For Love of the Duke
More than a Duke
The Love of a Rogue
Loved by a Duke
To Love a Lord
The Heart of a Scoundrel
To Wed His Christmas Lady
To Trust a Rogue
The Lure of a Rake
To Woo a Widow
To Redeem a Rake
One Winter with a Baron
To Enchant a Wicked Duke
Beguiled by a Baron
To Tempt a Scoundrel

To Hold a Lady's Secret
To Catch a Viscount
Defying the Duke
To Marry Her Marquess
The Devil and the Debutante
Devil by Daylight

THE HEART OF A SCANDAL

In Need of a Knight—Prequel Novella
Schooling the Duke
A Lady's Guide to a Gentleman's Heart
A Matchmaker for a Marquess
His Duchess for a Day
Five Days with a Duke

LORDS OF HONOR

Seduced by a Lady's Heart
Captivated by a Lady's Charm
Rescued by a Lady's Love
Tempted by a Lady's Smile
Courting Poppy Tidemore

SCANDALOUS SEASONS

Forever Betrothed, Never the Bride
Never Courted, Suddenly Wed
Always Proper, Suddenly Scandalous
Always a Rogue, Forever Her Love
A Marquess for Christmas
Once a Wallflower, at Last His Love

SINFUL BRIDES

The Rogue's Wager
The Scoundrel's Honor
The Lady's Guard
The Heiress's Deception

THE WICKED WALLFLOWERS
The Hellion
The Vixen
The Governess
The Bluestocking
The Spitfire

THE THEODOSIA SWORD
Only For His Lady
Only For Her Honor
Only For Their Love

DANBY
A Season of Hope
Winning a Lady's Heart

THE BRETHREN
The Spy Who Seduced Her
The Lady Who Loved Him
The Rogue Who Rescued Her
The Minx Who Met Her Match
The Spinster Who Saved a Scoundrel

LOST LORDS OF LONDON
In Bed with the Earl
In the Dark with the Duke
Undressed with the Marquess

BRETHREN OF THE LORDS
My Lady of Deception
Her Duke of Secrets

THE READ FAMILY SAGA
A Winter Wish

MEMOIR: NON-FICTION
Uninterrupted Joy

CHAPTER 1

London, England
Spring 1829

Wynn Masterson, the Marquess of Exmoor, and former Earl of Astor, had *always* been unfailingly respectable.

When other boys at first Eton and then Oxford had been off carousing, solidifying their reputations as some of London's wickedest scoundrels, he'd been steadfast in his studies, and careful with his consumption of spirits. After university, he'd only kept membership at White's and Brooke's, never frequenting the more scandalous hells favored by the rogues and rakes of Polite Society.

But sometimes being proper and doing all the right things didn't mean that trouble forever avoided you.

Sometimes, no matter how dutiful a son you were, or how dependable an estate owner and nobleman, the worst just happened.

For most any other gentleman, the public rejection of his marriage proposal—in the midst of it—would have been a worst thing.

And the fact it happened not once, but twice, by two different women in the exact same way, would certainly have qualified as that worst thing.

But even *that* was not the worst thing.

Nor, for that matter, had society learned of the very worst.

Not yet.

Years ago, there'd not been an urgency for him to wed.

Now, however? Now there was.

Wynn stared into the contents of his nearly empty snifter.

He'd never been much of a drinker. Certainly not a heavy one. Never had he descended into the level of debauchery found at the seedier establishments where men got soused beyond the point of reason.

He grimaced.

But then, no previous situation had merited spirits as this one did. If society thought Wynn being thrown over when he was bent on a knee proposing to a lady was scandalous, what would they say if—when—it was discovered, that Alice, the eldest of his unmarried sisters was in fact, with child.

Nay, he knew precisely what they would say. Just as he knew what the implications would be for his other unmarried sister. There'd be no union for her—at least, not one that was good or respectable. And there'd be few prospects for Wynn, who was tasked with producing an heir and seeing his mother and sisters cared for.

Restlessly, he swiped up the glass and finished the remaining amber contents.

With a grimace, he set the empty snifter down hard, thought better of it, grabbed the nearby bottle, and poured.

At the absolute worst time, the door opened, and his mother sailed in. Not even the faintest hint of grey peppered her black hair, nor a wrinkle marred her face. But then, he and her two daughters had never given reason to age her prematurely.

Until now.

The Dowager Marchioness of Exmoor shut the door behind her and joined Wynn at his desk.

She took the seat opposite him and with pain-filled eyes, she looked at his glass. "You're drinking."

It would have been worse had there been condemnation and not this sad disappointment.

"The situation does call for it," he muttered. It called for an entire bottle.

His mother eyed those spirits for a moment, and then leaning over, availed herself of his glass. She downed the contents without so much as a grimace, set the snifter down, and then sighed. "It didn't help."

His lips twitched. If he were capable of smiling, this would have been a moment. "No."

Her gaze slid to the newspaper, and she picked those pages up. "*This* is what they write of." She skimmed those handful of sentences there; ones he'd already committed to memory.

Scandal

Lord E was rejected—for a second time. Not unlike, when his previous marriage proposal was interrupted by the Duke of C, this time, it was interrupted by the Duke of G. Rumor has it, Poor Lord E was on a knee when this latest rejection came…

"I was so very certain she'd accept your offer and..." With a sigh, her words trailed off, and she gave her head another one of those regretful little shakes. "If they think *this* is a Masterson scandal..."

Wait until Alice's circumstances were discovered. When a young lady, without the benefit of marriage, found herself carrying a babe, as his eldest sister did, nothing but ruin awaited her—and her family. For who'd wed their daughter to Wynn? A man who'd proven himself unable to look after his female relatives, and whose family would forever carry a scandal with them for it.

Just like that, a familiar guilt hit him square in the gut. As soon as he'd learned Alice was with child, he'd done everything in his power to make his family's situation better. In finding a wife, he could have at least ensured the family line was secure.

"Wynn," his mother said quietly, pulling him back from his musings. "I did not mean to imply that Lady Lettie's rejection of your suit is not tragic in its own right."

He waved off that apology. At this point, everything was secondary to his sister. "I'm sure I could have done something differently. I should have offered for Lady Lettice soon—"

"Oh, hush," his mother chastised. "You were kind. Respectful. You brought her flowers. Everyone is talking about *you* now, and it is not in a good way." Her eyes flashed, as only a mama offended on behalf of her child could.

It had been hard finding a bride before. Now that he'd been made a laughingstock, it would be next to impossible. The truth of it was...women sought more than kindness and respectful. They sought passion and excitement, and well, he'd never been the rogue or rake.

"For what it is worth,"—*absolutely nothing*—"I wasn't on my knee the first time," he said with a feeble attempt at humor. The first time had come years earlier, when he'd paid a visit to Lady Daisy, the now Duchess of Crawford, intending to court the lady. "Only the second."

As intended, his mother managed the first smile he recalled in days.

Wynn grimaced. "Either way, it's no one's fault. It is just…bad luck." The fact that Wynn's sister had given her heart to an undeserving cad. The fact that her consummation of that relationship had resulted in a child. *All of it.*

"Bad luck." His mother's forlorn little voice confirmed she'd grasped what he was really speaking about. "Bad luck, indeed."

Alice's circumstances were the real tragedy here and not the fact that Wynn was being gossiped about.

"You did your best, Wynn," his mother said with a note of resignation. Tears sprung behind her eyes, and she looked away quickly, attempting to hide that glassy sheen.

Wynn glanced down at the newspaper, once more, his gaze unseeing the words about himself, his mind fixed on the only place it had been for the past four weeks.

Nausea churning in his belly, Wynn grabbed his decanter and poured himself that next drink his mother had previously interrupted. He took a deep swig.

After his mother composed herself, she resumed speaking. "You must not feel badly for the way things went with Lady Lettice." She sailed to her feet. "Now, we must be brave. The girls will need that. Especially Alice. I should begin the travel plans. Fortunately, Scotland is lovely this time of year."

His family's flight from Town had always been the expected solution. He'd just expected to have a respectable wife along with him when he joined the family's extended trip.

"Mother," he called when she started across the room.

She paused at the center of his office and glanced back.

"I will set the family to right." He had to.

"You need to worry about your own happiness."

He couldn't be happy unless she and his sisters were.

"Perhaps this is for the best," she said, with an eternal optimism only she could muster even in the most dire of situations.

"Oh?" he asked, because this, he really needed to hear.

"I was supportive of you courting Lady Lettice, when perhaps I shouldn't have been. I understood why you felt the match was the right one; she's the sister of a powerful marquess whose family is linked to a number of even more powerful families—Lord Rutland's. Lord Tennyson's. Each of whom had a scandal of their own, and not only braved it, but overcame it. Why, your thinking was so very logical…downright perfection."

He inclined his head. "Thank—"

"On the surface," she interrupted. "But if you married Lady Lettice, you would have denied yourself a union with a woman who truly wants you, who truly loves you as *you* deserve. And if I cannot have that for all of my children,"—*Alice*—"I'd have it for you, dear boy."

"My falling in love is irrelevant," he said wearily. Love solved nothing. Seeking a wife had never been about love.

"I believe you believe that," she said.

She couldn't possibly believe anything mattered more to him than securing their family. He opened his mouth to say as much but saw something in her eyes—an agonized glimmer, one that indicated how very desperate she was to find some good in any of this. Wynn forced a smile. "Mother."

A knock sounded at the door, and they instantly went silent.

His mother gave him a frantic look. Even whispering about it as they had, they'd risked the wrong staff member potentially overhearing and in turn bandying that salacious gossip about. It would be calamitous.

"Enter," he called.

The maid, Florence, ducked her head inside the room. "My pardon, my lord. I've been informed Lady Alice appears ill." She directed that to the dowager marchioness.

To his mother's credit, she appeared as in control as she had when Wynn and his sisters had fallen sick through the years, and she herself had helped care for them. "I'll be along shortly."

The moment the young girl dipped a curtsy and closed the door behind her, Wynn's mother looked to him. "I know you wished to find a bride before...*before*...but we must leave soon. How much longer will we be able to conceal the true reason for her on again, off again nausea?" she whispered, her words nearly inaudible.

"Soon," he promised. They'd leave for Scotland where Alice would be away from prying eyes.

His mother perked up. "Perhaps no one will assume anything. Society well knows her affinity for art. She's traveled several times before with this same purpose."

"Not during the Season," he gently reminded her. No marriage-aged lady left Town in the middle of a London Season, unless there was scandal chasing her away.

His mother drew in a shaky breath. "I should begin seeing to the preparations, my boy," she said.

Wynn stood and dropped a bow. "Mother."

The moment she'd gone, shutting that oak panel, he sank back into his chair. He dropped his forehead onto the desk, hitting it with a hard *thunk*.

"Does that help?" a voice called into the quiet, bringing his head shooting up so quickly, the muscles of Wynn's neck wrenched in painful protest. "If so, I dare think I should try it."

His sister, Alice, hovered at the side entrance of the room, a small smile on her lips.

He immediately jumped to his feet and rushed around the desk. "The maid said—"

She waved him off. "The maid made more of it than there is. I'm not an invalid, Wynn."

Nay, she wasn't an invalid. She'd always been an expert horsewoman, sailing over jumps that would have terrified the most seasoned riders. Scaling fallen trees when she'd been younger.

And as life would have it...scaling the tree outside her window to meet a man she'd no place meeting. A man whose intentions had not been honorable. And who'd left Alice—and their family—to deal with the consequences of that entanglement.

"Well, you didn't say?" Alice asked, dropping into the same chair their mother had occupied. "Does it help when dealing with a bad situation?"

"Which part? The cursing or hitting one's head?"

"Either."

"Alas, I am afraid neither." Nothing could help on that score.

They shared a smile.

And it felt normal for a moment. It felt like she was the same younger sister whom he'd taught to fish and ride, and as though she was not now the woman whose reputation hung in the balance, and because of it, the reason their entire family faced ruin.

Alice's gaze fell to Wynn's half-empty snifter. Her smile faded. "I was not sad about the news."

He stared dumbly at her. Surely, she wasn't saying—

"About Lady Lettie."

Oh. That made more sense. Wynn forced himself to grin. "Why, thank—"

"Not because she wasn't perfectly lovely, but because you didn't love her."

It had never been about love with Lady Lettice Brookfield. He couldn't say as much to his sister. Not without making her feel guilt he'd not have her feel.

"It *should* have been about love, Wynn," Alice said.

She'd always been too astute.

"Love found you…in the way you find yourself," he pointed out, gently, without recrimination.

Alice bit down on her lower lip. "He will come for me, you know."

Wynn knew no such thing. The only information he or their mother were in possession of was the fact Alice had lost her heart to a man without prospects, who'd gone to make a better life for himself—for them—and that he'd return. Only, he hadn't, and given the fact Alice's notes to the gentleman had gone unanswered, it was increasingly likely he never would.

Alice drew in a shaky breath. "I don't want you to feel guilty. Mother is right. This is not your fault, nor your responsibility."

He tensed. She'd been listening at the keyhole. At least no one else had. "Alice," he said gently. "I'm the marquess. You and Mother and our sisters are in fact my—"

"I don't want to be your responsibility," she repeated, a second time, more forcefully; her eyes snapped with the spirit of rebellion. "I don't want to be *anyone's* responsibility." In other words, she'd wanted to be loved. He wanted to kill the dastard, and never had he regretted there wasn't a second born son, so that Wynn could have avenged Alice as she deserved.

His sister looked as though she wished to say more, but without another word, left.

Wynn sat staring at the door of his office long after she'd gone with only one question repeating in his mind: what now?

CHAPTER 2

London, England
Spring 1829

Lady Caroline Brookfield had had a five-year reprieve.

She should have expected it would come to an end.

And yet, there'd been a whole four other children to occupy a dowager marchioness with marital machinations to last almost a decade: two sons—Miles, the Marquess of Guilford and Rhys the Rogue—long since reformed. The dowager also had two daughters: Rosalind, and the youngest of all Caroline's siblings, Lettie.

Why, there were even two granddaughters to occupy the dowager—Faith and Violet—Caroline's nieces—one who'd just had a Come Out and the latter who'd several years left before she made her debut. Surely two lovely, spirited granddaughters to marry off would be enough to occupy the dowager marchioness?

With all those children and grandchildren combined in need of making matches, it had been so very easy to believe that her mother might forget such similar—also unrealistic—plans for Caroline.

She'd been wrong. So very wrong.

Caroline tried to breathe.

After all, the dowager marchioness never, ever responded well to displays of temper.

Caroline studied her embroidery frame and made herself drag the tip of the needle through the fabric. Since the Scandal We Do Not Speak of, as her mother had referred to it, Caroline had developed an affinity for the previously hated-by-her, *task*. Tedious. Dull. As a girl, she'd once mocked the lauded ladylike activity. As a young woman who'd had her heart broken and been shamed in the most humiliating way, she'd found a peace in the pastime.

One didn't have to look a person in the eyes and see the pity or scorn or shame.

One could pretend to be riveted to the point of preoccupation and be spared those glances—or worse—discussions from concerned siblings about the changes time had wrought to her.

Caroline continued dragging the needle through the frame, her gaze locked on the sunny yellow threads coming together to form the bright outer circle of a cheerful sunflower.

"...it will do you good, Caroline," her mother was saying. "It has been long enough."

Keep even.

Keep calm.

Keep staid.

I am now the calm, dull, boring sister. Certainly capable of those feats perfected through the years.

Alas, there was no distracting herself from her mother. When the dowager marchioness was insistent, no one escaped whatever plans she'd hatched.

"I have taken part in the London Season," Caroline murmured evenly. "Countless ones." So many since the moment of her greatest shame.

There, the words sounded calm and steadily delivered.

From where she sat on the opposite sofa attending her own embroidery, her mother scoffed. "Do not be ridiculous," she said, not so much as pausing in her own efforts. "You did so as a companion to your sisters who've since each made a respectable match."

Caroline winced.

A respectable match.

It was what she'd accepted long ago she'd not have.

After all, ladies with scandalous pasts were not granted those gifts.

"Now, my dear, it is your time."

Caroline pushed the needle through with too much force; she jabbed her finger. A lone crimson droplet oozed to the skin.

Agatha, her dutiful maid—more friend these years than servant—was immediately on hand.

With a word of thanks, Caroline set the frame aside, accepted the kerchief, and pressed the white fabric against her smarting finger.

"My goodness, Caroline, you are never sloppy," her mother chastised.

No, she wasn't. She'd made a show of being anything but flawless through the years. She'd maintained a perfect demeanor in all things and in all ways, because the one time she'd been sloppy and free it had cost her mightily.

"Perhaps Aunt Caroline just required some red for her embroidery," her otherwise silent-until-now niece, Faith, called over from her place at the window seat.

Caroline flashed a grateful look to the younger woman. The two shared a grin.

"Do not be ridiculous, Faith," said the dowager marchioness, incapable of detecting sarcastic humor if it were a sharp-fanged monster who'd bit her square on the nose. "Your aunt would use red thread if that were the case."

"Of course," Faith rejoined with an impressively deadpan expression to match her tones.

Despite the misery of this dreaded exchange, Caroline managed another smile.

Over the years, her siblings had all gone their respective ways; finding love and happiness and starting families of their own. As such, it had been so much easier and so very comfortable to form a closer bond with her brother's adopted children. She often viewed them as the daughters she'd never have.

Perhaps her mother was letting the matter go. Perhaps, together, Caroline and Faith had diverted her attention enough—

"It is your turn, Caroline," her mother said impatiently.

Ah, she should have expected. When the dowager marchioness was bent on marrying a child off, not even Satan himself, engulfing the room around them with flames, could shake her from the topic.

"I am more than content, Mama, with my life," she murmured. Though she'd once dreamed of more than 'content'. She'd dreamed of grand passion and undying love and well, all those wishings had brought her nothing but trouble. Pierce, pull, push. She focused on the distracting cadence of those movements. "As it is, there is Faith's turn. Faith hardly needs her spinster aunt during her first Season."

"Do not be ridiculous, Aunt Caroline," Faith scoffed.

"I should love it dearly if you were there with me."

"See, there you have it," her mother said, lowering her embroidery frame to deliver a slight clap of her hands.

Caroline dug in. "Ah, but I can be with you, and not… not…be…" Searching for a husband. She couldn't make herself say it.

Because it made the dowager's intentions real and the situation imminent. Her poor mother truly thinking Caroline could have a normal, respectable match.

"You are no spinster, Aunt Caroline."

"What do you call a twenty-eight-year-old unmarried woman?" she asked, waggling her brows.

A slow, mischievous grin drew slowly up on the corners of her niece's lips. "Clever."

Despite herself, and despite the misery of this entire topic, a sharp bark of laughter burst from Caroline's lips, instantly earning a scowl from her mother.

"Young ladies do not snort, Caroline. You know that."

Yes, she did. Just as she knew young ladies who'd secretly gone about meeting a dashing rogue with less than honorable intentions did not then go on to make respectable matches. They only went on to make gossip for bored members of the peerage, who'd just been more successful than she at concealing their wickedness.

Giving up the pretense of caring about her embroidery, she laid the frame on her lap. "I'm not interested in having a formal season, and I'm less interested in making a match."

In a rare display of pique, the dowager slammed down her frame. "Are you destined and determined to be a poor relation dependent upon your brother's charity?"

Faith gasped. "Grandmere."

The dowager ignored her eldest grandchild. "Because

that is what you will be if you do not get over this ridiculous idea of yours that you'll not marry."

Tipping up her chin, Caroline held her mother's gaze. "Need I remind you of the reasons I will not marry?" The least of which had to do with it being a decision on her part. "Because if you need me to help you recall—"

Her mother paled. "Do not," she yelped, wagging a finger at Caroline. "I know...I know..." She oscillated her attention between her daughter and the things she wished to say, and her granddaughter, whom in front of, she could not.

There'd been any number of times over the course of Caroline's life where she'd been grateful for the companionship and friendship of her nieces. But this certainly ranked among the highest of those moments.

At last, the dowager sucked in a telltale, steadying breath between her slightly askew teeth. "The matter is settled, Caroline. There is no reason you can't and won't marry. It will be done." With actions to match the finality of that pronouncement, the dowager stood and took her leave.

Click.

The moment she had gone, and they were alone, Faith snapped shut whatever book she'd been reading. She jumped to her feet and joined Caroline. "You really are no burden, you know, Aunt Caro," Faith said in almost-angry tones.

In a world where she'd been used most shamefully by a fortune hunter, then ridiculed by the Ton for those mistakes, and then invisible to those same people who found different gossip to stew in, it was so very wonderful to know someone should be offended on her behalf.

Her throat worked, and Caroline stared down at her niece's ink-stained fingertips, covering that endearingly imperfect palm with her own. "Thank you, Faith," she said past a thick throat.

Even as her brother and his wife had proven gracious and only warm and welcoming, Caroline *felt* like a burden. Ultimately no married husband and wife truly wished to have a spinster sister about. Not when they were already suffering the misery of an unwanted dowager underfoot.

"And Grandmere is wrong…you do not *have* to marry." Faith paused, and Caroline glanced up. "If you, however, want to marry, then you should do that, too."

Want to marry.

"My days for that have come and gone." Caroline made herself say for her niece's benefit. Lying was easier than telling Faith the truth—all those years ago she'd been so very desperate to marry she'd believed the glib tongue and sweet words of a charlatan, a man who'd wished for her dowry. Ultimately, Miles had refused to relinquish those funds should they marry, insisting that Caroline keep them, he'd passed her over.

"They don't have to be," Faith said. "There are many respectable men out there. Good ones. Honorable ones."

A wistful smile toyed with Caroline's lips. The girl spoke with an insistence that only her tender years and innocence allowed.

"It's true," Faith pressed. "Why, Aunt Lettie even managed to find two of them."

The smile froze on her face. Yes, Lettie had found two of them. One a duke who loved her desperately. And the other a marquess, who'd been everything Faith now spoke of. Honorable, respectable. A good son and brother. No, men such as the Marquess of Exmoor didn't go marrying the sullied sister. They courted the spirited, still-pure one.

Faith touched a finger to Caroline's sleeve. "Aunt Caro?" she murmured, pulling Caroline back from those pathetic self-musings. "I've something for you."

Her niece hesitated, stealing a glance about the room. Her gaze lingered on Caroline's maid tucked away still in the corner, busy at work on an embroidery of her own.

Faith scooted closer.

Furrowing her brow, Caroline waited expectantly.

Her niece fished into the pocket sewn along the front of her day dress and withdrew something. Holding her fist up before Caroline's eyes, the girl slowly unfurled her fingers, revealing…a flash of gold.

Bending her head, Caroline stared at the pretty piece. Not the ornate diamonds and heavily jewel-studded pendant favored by the dowager, but simple and somehow familiar.

"My mother wore it," the girl murmured, seemingly following the direction of Caroline's thoughts. "As did my friend Marcia." Marcia as in the latest Diamond of the Season who'd gone from jilted at the altar to married to a viscount in what all society knew as one of those lucky, though rare, love matches.

"It is lovely," Caroline said.

"It is just not just lovely. It is…magic."

Caroline laughed, before registering the somber set to her niece's pretty features.

She was serious.

"Some women need magic. Some don't. Aunt Lettie did not."

Her niece wasn't wrong on that score. Some women did need magic to have even remotely happy lives. But magic wasn't real, and so their misery was, too.

"I take it I am one of those ladies requiring magic," she said dryly.

"Yes." Her niece spoke with an automaticity only a frank, honest young girl was capable of. "Me, too."

Faith made to press the piece on her, but Caroline gently pushed the girl's hands back. "What kind of aunt would I be if I stole magic from my niece who is so very deserving of it? Hmm?" Even if magic were real and it could bring Caroline the happily-ever-after she'd wished for, she'd not be so selfish as to take it from her niece, who found herself a wallflower through no crimes of her own—as Caroline did—but because of a small-minded society who could not see past the girl's partial deafness.

"You would be a wise aunt who realizes I'm really just seventeen, and not so very eager to rush into marriage." Faith paused. "For the moment, I am quite content waiting if it means you can be happy."

Tears smarted behind Caroline's eyes. "I am happy, poppet," she said thickly, palming her niece's cheek.

"Happi*er*, then," Faith corrected. She wagged a finger with a determination even the dowager would have been hard pressed to not admire. "And I shan't take no for an answer." With that, she looped the thin gold chain around Caroline's neck.

The moment the heart-shaped pendant fell into place against her chest, heat radiated from the point where the warm metal touched her.

Reflexively, Caroline touched a finger to the piece.

"There." Faith popped up from her seat. "It is done." With that, the younger girl skipped back across the room and returned to whatever work it was that occupied her that day.

Caroline pressed her palm against the necklace a second

time.

It is done.

There were no truer words spoken about Caroline's fate and future than those; different than what her niece had meant with those intentions, but no less real.

It had been done.

Caroline had been ruined long ago.

And no loving marriage to a respectable gentleman awaited her.

That was, without a hefty dose of the magic her niece had spoken of so innocently and optimistically.

CHAPTER 3

While Wynn's world burned, he sipped champagne and watched the young misses in the market for a husband.

It was perhaps the most English thing ever. Aside from tea and rain, of course.

And had he been capable of laughter, the absurdity of it all merited a good, hearty, healthy guffaw.

To his mother's and sister's credits, they wore their usual sincere smiles and chatted effortlessly with various guests throughout the Duke and Duchess of Crawford's ballroom.

A surfeit of guests.

The room was a crush of bodies with so many people crammed into the well-respected, and even more, well-liked, couple's ballroom that Wynn felt as if he were suffocating. His cravat tightened until he wanted to rip at the thing, yank it free and breathe more easily.

His gaze locked on his sister, Alice, some five or so paces away, conversing with the new Viscountess Waters. Color bloomed in Alice's cheeks as she happily engaged the other woman. Just then, the pair laughed at something; Alice's shoulders shook as did the viscountess's, and the other woman took Wynn's sister's hands and they leaned into one another. For all the world, they seemed innocent young ladies sharing a private jest, neither with a care in the world.

Only that wasn't the case.

At least, not for one of those young ladies.

For Alice, the world blazed too.

And there was absolutely no way this ended…except badly. An unmarried woman couldn't afford most scandals, but one of this nature? One so very permanent.

His throat constricted, and he reflexively grabbed a spare glass of champagne from a passing servant's tray and downed it in one long, slow swallow.

"I expected more people to be talking about you and staring," an amused voice sounded just over his shoulder.

Wynn's fingers tightened on the thick stem of his crystal flute as he looked blankly at the grinning guest who'd joined him.

Alaric Casterleigh, the Earl of Denbigh, Wynn's closest friend since Eton—his only real friend, and as close to him as his own siblings. Yet Wynn hadn't breathed a word about Alice even to him. Which begged the question… what did he know? His mouth dry; his palms suddenly wet, Wynn tried to strangle out a greeting.

Denbigh's usual grin faded, and his features grew serious, concerned. "Bloody hell, man, I was attempting to make light. Not a person would blame you. That is, not a reasonable person. You've nothing to be embarrassed over. The lady simply married another. That is no reflection upon you."

The lady simply married another?

And then it hit Wynn; the conclusion his friend had drawn, and relief swept through him. "I...thank you for that."

The earl snorted. "For what? Being your friend? It's really no chore."

Which wouldn't be the case when it was discovered Alice was with child. Not that he believed the earl would abandon his support of Wynn and his family. Neither did he intend to divulge that most personal of secrets his sister possessed to anyone.

Wynn made a show of examining the dance floor.

How singularly strange that the one great worry Wynn had, the peril Alice, and subsequently his other sisters and their mother faced, should be his only thought, and the world remained ignorant of their turmoil. At least, for now they did.

Soon...

Wynn grabbed another glass of champagne from a servant who came to collect his empty one and proceeded to sip, this time more slowly.

All the while, he was aware of his friend's probing stare. "I don't believe I've ever seen you down spirits in quite this way," he remarked quietly, casually drinking from his own glass. "I trust to some surprise. I didn't know your heart was so engaged. I should have expected differently. You are not one to marry where there isn't some strong regard felt."

This was safer. Denbigh believing Wynn's distraction stemmed from his recent rejection by Lady Lettice Brookfield. And yet, it also felt wrong to let his friend believe he'd truly loved Lady Lettie. He hadn't. He'd respected her. She'd been witty and clever, and yet—

"I'm thirty-five years old, Denbigh. I have sisters and a

mother reliant upon me and it has..." he considered his words carefully a moment "...occurred to me more frequently that were something to happen to me—"

"Nothing is going to happen to you," his friend interrupted.

"But if it does, the line passes to a distant relative. A nice enough chap, but also one who barely knows my mother and sisters, and whom I cannot say with any real confidence will take care of them as they need or deserve."

"So you marry another," Denbigh said, as if it were the easiest thing in the world.

And honestly, in London, the capital of the marriage mart with young women and their mamas dedicated to making a match, it should be. That hadn't proven the case for Wynn.

"Alas," he drawled. "There aren't a whole number of ladies throwing their gloves in my path."

"Then find one of the ones whose long past throwing their gloves. Someone mature and respectable, as yourself." Denbigh made a vague gesture about the room at large, pulling Wynn's gaze out. "Someone, say, with a similar history of your own."

Wynn froze. His gaze locked on a stoic lady standing across the room; flanked by her brother and sister-in-law. The woman looked for all the world bored; almost pained to be here. As only a lady who'd also found herself courted and then passed over numerous times, could.

None other than Lady Beatrice Dennington.

Declared a diamond at her debut, the late Duke of Somerset's daughter had been sought after by countless gentlemen, all of who'd ultimately pivoted and wed different ladies. She'd been thrown over for another so many times the lady had been talked about in unkind ways. Not to her face, of course. Society would never cut a duke's daughter or sister.

Wynn froze.

Of course, why hadn't he thought of it?

Not unlike Lady Lettie, Lady Beatrice was mature, and she not only came from one of the most respectable families in England, her brother's marriage to a gaming hell bookkeeper had given them even greater influence. A different kind of influence. But no less important. That hadn't always been the case for the Dennington family.

His mind raced. Having been herself a subject of whispers because of her familial connections to the Hell and Sin club, the lady had proven herself indifferent to the opinions of the haute Ton. She'd held her head high at every function; until Polite Society had grown bored and Lady Beatrice's link to that hell had become just another afterthought about her. Such a woman would surely not be cruel and unforgiving to Wynn's sister.

He silently, hurriedly tabulated. Lady Beatrice must be on her…seventh? Eight? Ninth Season? As such, perhaps she'd be more amenable to a match not with a young charmer, but rather with someone who was safer and possessed of an honorable reputation.

"You're a genius, Denbigh" Wynn whispered.

Denbigh flashed a cheeky grin. "It's commonly known." He lifted his glass in a small salute, touching the edge of it against Wynn's. The crystal clinked in a cheerful way.

Wynn had believed his family's situation futile; he'd resigned himself to the fact that he'd not find a respectable wife before his sister's situation was discovered. And for the first time in a very long time, something blossomed in his chest—hope.

Perhaps there was still a chance for him and his family,

after all.

Suddenly, the Duke and Duchess of Crawford's ball didn't seem like such a terrible place to be.

CHAPTER 4

At the Duke and Duchess of Crawford's ball, on display before Polite Society was the last place Caroline wished to be.

Caroline, the pathetic spinster who'd fallen prey to a fortune-hunter years earlier, and who now proved foolish enough to believe she could find a husband. Or that was how the papers were writing of her, anyway.

It had been one thing when she was the invisible companion, sitting in the shadows while her sisters and niece made their come-outs. It was an altogether different matter when Caroline dared to present herself as a marital candidate. It didn't matter that her mercenary-when-it-came-to-proper-unions mother was in fact the one behind Caroline's *efforts*.

Yes, at *that* moment, she'd become the favorite topic for those gossips to cut their teeth on.

"Are you all right, Aunt Caroline?" Faith whispered. "You look unwell."

Unwell?

Caroline wanted to vomit, and if she'd had any contents in her stomach, she suspected she would have.

She offered her niece a wan smile. "I'm—"

"Of course, she is fine." The dowager marchioness snapped out that response for Caroline. "Why shouldn't she be?"

"Why, indeed?" Caroline gritted out, and she and her niece shared a look. And for that matter, why should Caroline dare offer an opinion as to her own well-being?

The younger girl looped her arm supportively through Caroline's, and never had she been more grateful for the friendship...at that, from her younger niece. "These are sad days indeed, when the niece offers her aging aunt comfort, and not the other way around."

Faith scoffed, giving her a light squeeze. "Oh, hush. You are not even yet eight and twenty."—Ancient by Polite Society's standards—"And why should I not be able to give my aunt support from Grandmere?"

Faith, and her sister Violet, had been the daughters she'd so very much wanted for herself. It was a dream Caroline had been forced to lay to rest; it'd died along with the virtue she'd cast away.

"He is here!"

From any other mother, those excited tones would be suited to the arrival of a beloved child or grandbabe. Not so from Caroline Brookfield's mother.

Where the Dowager Marchioness of Guilford was concerned, the absolute and only object befitting that manner of eagerness was—a potential bridegroom.

Caroline looked to the front of the receiving line, her gaze lingering on Lord and Lady Ambrose assembled in wait. The notoriously lecherous viscount was eighty if he was a day, while his wife was nearer in age to Caroline.

The gaunt young woman appeared haggard. Miserable.

That is the fate that awaits me—and only if I'm lucky—the arm ornament and brooding mare for some ancient gentleman.

"Did you hear me, Caroline?" her mother asked impatiently, baldly staring at the receiving line. "I said he's arrived!"

"I'm fairly certain the gentleman isn't in the market for a wife. Lord Ambrose's wife looks to be in perfectly fine health."

And thank goodness for that. Otherwise, there was a certainty Caroline's match-minded mama would have finagled a meeting between her and the old lord.

Her mother frowned. "Jests do not suit you, Caroline."

"I disagree," Faith interjected with her usual loyalty and absolute fearlessness of the dowager marchioness. "I rather prefer Aunt Caro cracking quips."

Caroline's mother—Faith's grandmother—pursed her mouth in a terrifying way. "Gentlemen do not prefer ladies who are *cracking quips*."

"Then I say we're better off without those stodgy sorts," Faith muttered, pulling an unexpected laugh from Caroline and another sharp, disapproving glare from her grandmother.

It was on the tip of Caroline's tongue to point out, gentleman—of either sort—didn't prefer ladies who were demure, as she'd learned first-hand. Or scandalous, as she'd become. But she didn't point that out, just as she didn't point out that she'd not been making a jest.

"Either way, I'm not speaking about Lord Ambrose. I'm speaking about *him*." With a discreet little point of her glove-encased finger, her mother motioned, and Caroline followed that gesture across the room, and to the line, and to the—

She froze.

Now her mother must be cracking quips and making jests because—

"You are not...*serious*," she whispered, her voice strangled, as Lord Ambrose totted on down the steps, with his wife on one arm, and his cane in the other hand.

"Do I appear as though I am jesting?" her mother murmured.

"Given Grandmere's position moments ago on gentlemen cracking quips," Faith drawled, "I daresay she's not one for ladies—even herself—making them."

"No," Caroline choked. "Just...no."

As in an absolute no.

That managed to draw her mother's less than discreet attention away from the gentleman and over to her daughter.

"No?" her mother retorted. "*Nooo?*"

Yes, a declination from Caroline was destined to be met with that extra emphasis, and additional three syllables the dowager marchioness somehow managed to squeeze into that single-word utterance.

"Caroline Rose Brookfield, did you just tell me... 'no'?"

Yes, the shock was merited. Following her ruin, Caroline had done absolutely everything within her power to be the dutiful daughter, conducting herself in an always agreeable way. She'd blackened her name so badly, she'd done everything after that above reproach.

Fat lot of good it had done her.

But this? This, Caroline drew the absolute line at. "No. I said, 'no', Mother," she said, quietly and firmly, proud of that steady delivery, and she focused on her mother's shocked features.

To Marry Her Marquess

Hmm. It appeared her younger sister Lettie had been correct, after all when she'd said it was best to turn the tables on their mother because it distracted her from whatever ruthless, mercenary thoughts rolled around that single-track mind. But her mother's attention was not on the gentleman now moving through the crowd, and the swarm of suitors converging on his sister.

Alas, her mother found Caroline—as she invariably did. "And whyever not," her mother demanded on a furious whisper.

"Whyever not?" Caroline echoed. "Because he almost married my sister." And he would have married her sister had Lettie not gone and fallen in love with the Duke of Lennox.

"Almost." Her mother lifted a single digit up towards Lord and Lady Wessex's mural overheard. "But he did *not*."

"You want me to marry a gentleman who carried a tendre for my sister?" she asked incredulously. Not 'carried'. He likely still *did* hold an affection for Lettie. Who wouldn't? Lettie was everything Caroline had once been—but with a flawless reputation, to boot.

"Hush," her mother scolded through a painfully tight smile, which Caroline swiftly donned, and they waved politely and inclined their heads as Lady Templeton passed.

The moment the matron was out of earshot, Caroline's mother turned back. "He did not marry your sister. And I would be remiss if I failed to point out that even your sister made a match."

Yes, because even her sister, whom the dowager marchioness had lamented and despaired of ever seeing wed because of her plainspoken ways and free spirit, had managed to snag a husband.

And a most powerful one, at that.

"And a most powerful one, at that," her mother finished the rote words she'd uttered ad nauseam.—*A duke*—"A duke."

If Caroline had less self-restraint, she'd have pulled a face at her mother's obsequious response.

"Lettie has done you a dear favor. For her wedding His Grace, means Lord Exmoor is perfectly available for you."

Her temper flared, and she could not contain her resentment, at her mother, for her circumstances, and the world at large. "And one Brookfield girl is the same as the next, eh?"

"Eh?" With her fan, her mother wrapped Caroline lightly on the top of her hand. "And for that matter, yes, it is all the same. The gentleman needs a wife, and any wife will do. Lettie is married and you should find hope in that."

She didn't.

Because Caroline was nothing like Lettie.

Lettie who openly laughed, and teased, and bantered, and in short, was an effortless conversationalist because she did not try.

On the other hand, Caroline, with her blackened reputation, had been forced to become something Lettie had never been:

Quiet.

Dull.

Boring.

Spiritless.

Until now.

Caroline drew the line at this.

Her mother gripped her wrist. "Now, come, let us—"

Caroline dug in her heels, bringing her mother to a grinding stop.

"Caroline?" The dowager marchioness looked back in abject confusion, blinking wildly, and staring concernedly down at her feet. "Whatever is wrong with your feet? They are not moving."

And they would not be. "I am not pursuing His Lordship."

A mottled color filled her mother's cheeks. "Of course, you are not." She paused. "You do not pursue anyone. The gentleman will pursue you."

"No, you misunderstand me—"

"He is coming," her mother whispered furiously. "Do hush."

And then it happened.

Her mother placed her palms on the small of Caroline's back and shoved hard.

Caroline saw it all in endlessly slow, agonizing motion as the marquess stepped closer.

The stunned surprise that filled Lord Exmoor's sharp features.

And then Caroline was coming down hard, landing even harder on her knees upon the marble floor.

Caroline lay there, sprawled like a babe who'd just learned to crawl, staring at boots and slippers.

With that, not for the first time in her existence, she found herself in the place she hated most—with all eyes upon her. *I'm going to throw up.* Even without looking up, she felt those stares. She who'd come to crave and love the invisibility that her reputation had earned her found herself the object of the crowd's focus.

Unblinking, she stared at the white-marble floor with its faint brown veins.

Her mother had insisted there was nothing more disastrous than being a lady still unwed after six entire Seasons.

She'd been wrong. So very wrong. There was something far worse.

And no, it wasn't that Caroline's mother, the Dowager Marchioness of Guilford, had hurled—literally hurled—her at a gentleman.

Why, it wasn't even that it was the *same* gentleman whom the dowager marchioness had employed such a technique with her younger daughter—who'd invariably wed another man.

Rather, it was the fact that where the Marquess of Exmoor had caught Caroline's sister, her mother's target this time proved poor, the gentleman's reflexes slower, and Caroline landed hard on her knees, before ultimately landing flat—and hard—on her stomach on the side of the Duchess of Crawford's ballroom dance floor.

Silence.

It was staggering and powerful and great.

It was also something Caroline had thought to be an impossibility in the midst of any well-attended Ton event.

And here it turned out the surefire and only way to silence society was when someone pushed a lady flat on her face.

If there were a Lord above, and he was a merciful one, he'd splay the floor open and let Caroline fall all the way through.

But he wasn't—either merciful or present. Mayhap both.

A pair of boots collided directly with her line of vision.

She knew those boots. Or at least, the wearer of them. She'd seen them time enough before.

"Stay down," her mother all but hissed that furious

whisper.

Stay down?

Oddly, that state—prone on the floor—was vastly preferable to taking her feet and facing down the sea of guests all singularly fascinated by this great humiliation.

And then, no doubt to her mother's delight, a hand appeared before Caroline's eyes.

A large, glove-encased, powerful palm.

She closed her eyes briefly. "I have it," she said, between tightly clenched teeth.

Her mother gasped. "Caroline!"

Yes, because pride, according to her mother, was one of the greatest sins. Pride in the face of a bachelor looking for a wife was a cardinal one.

Only, in this instant, Caroline didn't give a damned about propriety. She could not accept that piteous offering.

Ignoring her mother's sputtering and the marquess's fingers that remained outstretched, Caroline struggled—and mightily—in her skirts to get herself upright. She pitched forward and another round of collective gasps went up throughout the ballroom. But this time, she managed to retain her footing.

Unable to tip her neck back and meet his eyes, Caroline kept her gaze squarely on the gentleman's cravat, and then with her knees smarting as they'd not smarted since she'd been a girl scaling trees a lifetime earlier, Caroline collected her hem, tipped her chin up, and with all the dignity she might muster, marched off through the crowd that parted like a sea to allow her to pass.

And then up and out of the ballroom.

CHAPTER 5

Wynn had oft excelled in athletic ventures.

He was a proficient rider, fencer, and boxer, having sparred regularly and with much success against even the famed Gentleman Jackson. In addition, there'd never been a tennis match or rapier fight he'd struggled at or with.

Nay, he wasn't the clumsy sort to go about faltering on his feet or dropping things.

Ladies on the other hand? *Ladies* he apparently dropped.

Though in fairness, he'd caught Lady Lettice Brookfield; the last lady shoved his way by the Dowager Marchioness of Guilford. Yes, Lady Lettice he'd caught. The woman he'd ended up courting who'd instead rejected his suit and married another.

The latest, however? The lady's sister?

No such luck there.

Bloody hell on Sunday.

He'd dropped her. Or, failed to catch her. Either way, the outcome had been the same.

Wynn, along with every other guest present, stared at the retreating lady and her mother fast at her heels.

Alice and Denbigh were on Wynn at the same time. "What just happened?" His sister's features and whisper reflected the same horror and shock to match his own.

"I...."

"Was not so fleet of hand this day," the earl drawled, and Wynn shot him an annoyed glance.

The other man flashed a grin and shrugged his shoulders. "What? You weren't."

No, in fairness, Wynn hadn't been.

It had all happened so very quickly. He'd been headed to request a set from Lady Beatrice. He'd been so singularly focused on his sudden purpose that he'd never in a million and one years have expected the Brookfield mother to have orchestrated the exact same attempt at capturing his notice with two daughters. And he'd not forget the sight of Lady Caroline sprawled face-first at his feet, or the stricken expression in her pretty features as he'd held out a hand.

I should have plucked her up...

His mother hurried over, joining their trio. "The gall of that woman," she seethed. "How dare she shove her daughter so."

Yes, it was the shrewish, mercenary dowager marchioness who bore the blame that day.

Knowing that, however, did not make Wynn feel any better or ease the way his chest muscles tightened.

"I for one think you should go after her," Alice said.

"That seems like a...possibly dangerous idea," his mother whispered.

Alice puzzled her brow. "Why?" she asked, with still an artful innocence.

"Oh, I don't know," Denbigh answered dryly. "Perhaps because the entire reason the lady's shrewish mother orchestrated that fall was so that the lady would catch your brother's notice, and in turn prompt him to marry the lady. What harm could possibly come to Exmoor in going off alone and seeking that lady out?"

Wynn's mother rang her hands. "Precisely. It is that, precisely."

Alice rolled her eyes. "La, how chivalrous of you, sir." She proceeded to launch into a lecture on chivalry and decency.

"Decency?" Denbigh challenged. "You'd be better served giving that lesson to the dowager marchioness."

Never had his sister and best friend missed an opportunity to spar. This, however, was not the time for it. Wynn resisted the urge to jam his fingertips into his temples. "Can we please, stop," he said tersely. "If I might belabor you to refrain from this particular discussion given the attention we're attracting."

As one, his mother, his sister, and best friend looked out.

Sure enough, every pair of eyes that had been previously trained on Lady Caroline and her flight had found their way back to Wynn.

Heat crept up his neck and climbed to his cheeks. Oh, how he despised attention being on him.

Mayhap that came from the fact that he'd never been the manner of fellow to snag the Ton's notice. Over the years, unfailingly, he'd conducted himself in a way that was above reproach. He'd not been a rogue and rascal whom stories followed. As such, people didn't generally stare at him or pay him any heed.

Or they hadn't, anyway.

"Wynn is right," his mother said quietly. "Let us stop quarreling." She looked pointedly at Denbigh and Alice who under that direct stare each dropped their gazes to the floor. "It makes sense for Alice—"

Alice's skin paled, and she swayed slightly.

Wynn cursed and made a rush to catch her arm, just as Denbigh did. "The heat," Alice whispered weakly, waving them off, and taking a deep breath.

"Yes, it is quite hot in here," their mother said so evenly that even Wynn almost believed it was the crush of the room and not Alice's condition which accounted for her reaction.

In their attempt to have Alice out and about to maintain the appearance of all things normal, they danced dangerously close to discovery.

"Perhaps you might be so good as to escort Alice for a glass of lemonade, Laurence," the dowager said. Hers may as well have been a battlefield order that neither Wynn nor any of his siblings, and certainly not his friend, had been able to deny over the years.

Denbigh dropped a bow, even as Alice groaned.

"But I don't *want* to sip lemonade with Denbigh."

The earl shot a hand to his breast. "You're wounding my ego, Al."

The marchioness cast a warning glance at her protesting daughter.

"Fine, I shall allow him to escort me, but I shan't like it," Alice vowed, even as she placed her fingertips atop the earl's sleeves and allowed him to escort her to an available seat.

The moment they'd gone, and the orchestra struck up the strains of the lively dance, Wynn's mother looked his way. "I am worried about the girl," she declared in hushed tones.

Wynn looked to Alice and Denbigh and his gut tightened. "Perhaps I should have the carriage summon—"

His mother waved off the remainder of his words. "I wasn't speaking about Alice. If we leave on a rush, that would attract more attention. I was referring to the other one." She gave a discreet but still pointed enough nod of her chin in the direction Lady Caroline had departed.

His stomach churned. "Oh." That girl who wasn't a girl, but rather a young woman, one whom he'd gotten on rather well with back when he'd been courting her sister. Lady Caroline had always been first to greet him while he'd waited for Lady Lettie to arrive, and who'd often spoken to him about whatever flowers he'd shown up with. She'd always been smiling.

His smile faded at a different memory, a more recent one from moments ago—the lady's stricken eyes; her high, proud cheekbones deathly pale then rapidly red.

And the memory of her sprawled at his feet hit him square in the chest. Wynn swept his gaze over the crowded ballroom. The guests' attention and interest in him had since faded as they'd moved their focus on in search of current, more salacious gossip than Wynn standing with his mother.

"Are you listening to me, Wynn?" his mother urged insistently.

No. "Yes."

"The dowager is desperate. That does not mean her daughter is. I saw the young lady. The last thing she was interested in was any attention from you."

"Why, thank you," he drawled.

"Oh, hush. It's not about you at this moment." She paused. "Not completely." His mother honed her gaze on

Lady Caroline's mother. "I am quite adept at dealing with Dorinda. In the event she's concocted some manner of scheme to see her daughter ruined by you, I'll ensure she's occupied while you verify the lady is unhurt. Be quick."

With that, she headed over to the mercenary mama in question. None would dare doubt the sincerity of his mother's smile. She spoke easily with Lady Caroline's mother as if it were the most natural thing in the world to strike up a chat with the woman who'd pushed her daughter into her son.

Wynn remained there several moments more, ensuring the dowager marchioness was suitably occupied then went in search of Lady Caroline.

CHAPTER 6

Caroline did not want to be found.

Not this day. Not any day. Not by anyone.

It was why, even with her knees smarting viciously from her impact a short while ago with the hard, unforgiving marble floor, Caroline ran.

She ran down the deserted halls, as fast and hard as she'd not remembered running, even back in her hoydenish days as a girl playing with her sisters. She ran with a speed she'd not believed herself capable of any longer.

Her breath came in sharp, noisy rasps as she went, her skirts hiked high above her ankles.

She ran as if in so doing, she might reverse the course of time, bring herself back to some different time and any different moment, other than the one that had just taken place.

But then, humiliation had that effect. It gave even the most proper lady like Caroline the ability to take flight.

She reached the glass terrace doors leading to a path out where freedom beckoned, and she lengthened her strides all the more.

Caroline paused only long enough to grab the handle push the panel wide and stagger outside. She shoved the door shut and resumed her race; sprinting down the length of the terrace until the balustrade rushed to meet her.

With a ragged gasp, her chest heaving and her sides aching from her exertion, Caroline slumped along the stone railing; she borrowed support from it and welcomed the sharp feeling in her breast from her run.

The pain was welcome for it proved a distraction from her earlier humiliation.

Alas, it provided only a brief distraction.

"Oh, God," she whispered, and hers was a prayer and plea to the Lord above, who'd not seen fit to open the stone floor and let her sink underneath as she'd begged of him that night.

Her mother had thrown her.

She'd actually hurled her at Lord Exmoor in the same exact fashion she'd shoved Caroline's sister, Lettie, at him.

But then, he'd caught Lettie.

Because Lettie was eminently catchable, and Caroline was entirely forgettable.

Shame, humiliation, and pain all warred for supremacy in her breast, ultimately creating a sharp blend of its own type of misery.

She squeezed her eyes shut.

Did I think he should have caught me?

I was never anything to him—just the spinster he graciously spoke with when he came to court my younger, more charming, more respectable sister.

And now, with Lettie having thrown him over and married a duke in his stead, Caroline was even less.

Caroline sucked in a ragged breath and passed her miserable gaze over the gardens below to the various statues of Greek gods and goddesses carved in stone, throughout—before her eyes snagged upon that chiseled rendering of Clementia, one arm extended as if she stretched a hand in mercy out to Caroline, and the other pointed skyward; from that place of which she drew her power.

Tears pricked her lashes; the moisture stinging and burning her eyes, and she wrenched her gaze away from that life-like statue, burying her face against the cool stone balustrade.

Caroline let her shoulders sag as the fight went out of her, and she gave in to the pain throbbing away at her legs.

This was to be her fate, then? Unmarried…and stuck with her miserable mother for the remainder of her days. A mother who never failed to point out her failings, or lament Caroline's unwed state, and remind her of the reasons she wasn't married.

And, well, Caroline knew she wasn't the interesting character her sisters, Lettie or Rosaline were and always had been, or charming as her brothers, but surely the fact that she was saddled with a mother like the dowager marchioness was enough to deter even the most stalwart gentleman.

With a painful sigh, she turned and stared out across the vast London sky. Distractedly, through her gown, she rubbed at her wounded knees and studied the thick, heavy rainclouds that rolled by overhead, blotting out the moon and allowing only the occasional star the faintest flicker in the night.

Only, if she were being truly honest with herself, it wasn't her mother who was to blame for being unmarried after six seasons.

It was Caroline.

Because Caroline had believed the pretty words and even prettier promises from a scoundrel. She had believed them so much that she'd traded her virtue and all hope of a respectable future for that gift. Those past sins were hard enough for any honorable man to overlook. To add a potential mercenary mother-in-law into the proverbial mix? Well, then Caroline had a greater chance of finding the end of a rainbow than a respectable husband.

Click.

The door opened.

Double damn.

Of course, her mother would not allow her even this solitude. Gritting her teeth, Caroline stopped rubbing at her legs and straightening, she turned and faced her mother.

"Will you not go away? Must—*You*," she murmured, that word leaving her on a breathy exhalation.

For it wasn't an enraged dowager marchioness.

It was the Marquess of Exmoor.

Even with only the lit braziers along the terrace some twenty paces away, she'd recognize him anywhere; a bold, angular jaw, with a slight indentation at the center the only hint of softness within the granite curvature. His cheeks were equally sharp and carved with strength those stone Greek gods below would have envied. "Forgive me," he said quietly. "I will—"

"No!" she exclaimed; her voice a rolling echo around the terrace. "I...forgive me. I thought you were another," she finished weakly.

She thought he might leave, anyway.

He should.

It was improper for him to be here.

And over the years, he'd garnered an illustrious reputation for doing what was proper. Unlike Caroline…

Lord Exmoor started forward his steps slow, as if allowing her a second time to order him gone, and she knew he would if she did.

Her heart hammered, and the misery in her legs was briefly forgotten as her mind honed in on one more important detail than the nagging ache of her injured knees—he was here.

Surely, she should only be consumed with the humiliating shame that accompanied the scene her mother had just made, and yet, it spoke to how pathetic Caroline was that she welcomed the sight of him anyway.

Why was he here?

Surely it was a coincidence.

For he'd certainly not seek her out. Not after all that had transpired between him and Caroline's sister, and certainly not after that scene in the ballroom.

And then, he stopped before her.

She didn't wish to see him.

Not that he could blame her.

From the corner of her strained eyes to her equally strained mouth—Wynn paused, his gaze lingering of its own volition upon that cherry-red flesh.

And he proved a bastard for the second time that night, for surely the only thing worse than failing to catch a lady when she fell was noting that indent at the upper side and a pointed tip at the lower which leant her lips a heart-shaped quality. It was a full, lush mouth that put all manner of wicked thoughts in the heads of even respectable men.

Wynn wrenched his gaze away, forcing it up a fraction to those glacial blue eyes that watched him guardedly.

"I came to see if you are well," he said quietly.

"Prodigiously so," she replied instantly. "I'm..." Her brow furrowed.

Wynn stared at her questioningly.

"Do you know, I'm not." She slashed a hand in the direction of the doorway. "My mother humiliated me." And then, she began to pace, her movements slightly uneven as she marched back and forth. "I snagged my hem," she pointed, and he followed the tip of her index finger to the dangling bit of lace. "My knees hurt, and I know I'm not supposed to mention my knees, because ladies don't talk about the human body."

A streak of lightning split across the night sky, bathing her features in the impending storm's glow. Her spirited rant lent her cheeks a fiery color that enhanced their beauty, and then her words, coupled with her strained features, hit him. That strain was a product of her hurt. "Nor am I so much as to mention the human body," she was saying, "which actually, I can now admit is really quite ridiculous as we are all humans and we all have knees, and mine hurt."

He stared on, completely enthralled by that fiery display.

Suddenly, she stopped, and the bold strokes of her cheekbones turned a heightened shade of red as she seemed to note his study. And then misunderstood the reason for it. "Forgive me," she said stiffly. "I should allow you to your company." She made to step around him, limping slightly.

Yes, their parting ways was best. He'd made his

apologies. There was really nothing more to do.

"Please," he said quickly, and Lady Caroline turned back.

Wynn motioned to a nearby stone bench.

She followed his gesture and then looked questioningly at him. "My lord?"

"I...would you allow me to see to your injury?"

The lady dampened her mouth. "It is," Lady Caroline dropped her voice to a whisper, "my legs."

He quirked his lips up in a wry grin. "Yes. A wise woman once pointed out how ridiculous it is we are forbidden from talking about the human body as we all have one."

A reluctant smile spread across her lips.

He saw her wavering and pressed her further. "I assure you, I'm not a gent to have designs upon a lady's knee. I've two sisters and as such, I'm quite familiar with scraped and exposed knees."

Lady Caroline's mouth twitched again, and this time she took a seat on the bench.

Wynn dropped to a knee beside her. "May I?" he murmured, gesturing to her.

Wordlessly, she nodded.

Wynn caught the edge of her satin skirts and slowly inched the fabric up.

With every hedonistic rustle of satin, he exposed her lower limbs, revealing her calves—sleek, muscled, and strong belonging to a woman who used them for riding—and it conjured delicious images. Shamefully wicked ones. Of these long, contoured limbs wrapped about his waist as he moved within her.

And...Lord help him, in that instant, he came to two discoveries all at once: one, he was not the honorable, respectable man he'd always prided himself on being, and two, not all knees were created equal. Nor for that matter had he considered in order to reach the lady's knee, he'd have to climb his gaze past the lower portion of her sheer stockinged leg.

"Is it…bad?" she ventured.

Bloody hell. This was very bad, indeed.

He swallowed. Or tried to. His tongue heavy and his mouth dry, that spasmodic motion proved suddenly next to impossible. "It is painful," he managed. "For you, I trust?" He wrenched his gaze upward, to find the lady staring down at him with her cheeks still pink and her eyes wholly unaffected. "I trust it is painful for you." *Of course it is painful.* She'd said as much, and it showed as much in the redness of that skin and the beginning black and blue beginning upon it.

And deuced if he wasn't the worst sort of cad for lusting after her this way.

Lady Caroline opened her mouth when behind her another bold streak of lightening zigzagged across the sky, even as simultaneously the skies opened up in a deluge. Long, angry slashes of rain hit the earth noisily, drops spraying periodically into his and her portion of the terrace.

Wynn hopped up and yanked a kerchief from his pocket. He dangled that fabric over the railing, and the rainwaters instantly soaked the stark white material. After ringing it out, he returned to the spot before Caroline, and falling to his haunches once more, he lightly pressed the cold cloth against her leg.

She gasped, and he quickly looked up. "Forgive me."

"It does not hurt," she hurried to assure him. "It is the c-cold." Her voice trembled.

That quaver he understood. He was shaken in that instant, too.

Wynn returned his attention to the task at hand. Forcing himself to think of it as a task, he periodically rotated the fabric after it had warmed some, to apply the colder portion. He did so several times. And as he did, it occurred to him that her mother would have loved nothing better than to come out and find him and Lady Caroline, so.

And it also occurred to him that he didn't give a damn if the archbishop himself took a stroll on the terrace and discovered Wynn with his hands on this woman.

This.

This right here was why discussions of the human body were forbidden. And why men didn't touch the legs of delectably lovely women.

Because it wasn't all so simple as, *everyone has limbs*.

Because no one, absolutely no one, had legs like this woman before him.

Wynn's fingers shook slightly.

He continued tending her and wanted to continue touching her so, and yet...even as a gentleman without a roguish reputation, he well-knew he played with fire, and the only one who'd be scorched by it were they to be discovered was this woman before him. Wynn looked up. "Any better?"

"Much, my lord," she said, with the widest, biggest most trusting blue eyes he'd ever seen. The kind of sparkling blue a fellow could drown within. How had he failed to note those shimmering pools of her blue eyes before?

"Wynn," he murmured, his gaze locked with hers, trapped there.

She cocked her head.

"That is, given…" *the fact I have your leg in my hand still* "…this evening…" he settled for that vagueness "…using our Christian names, seems more appropriate."

The lady hesitated. "You may call me, Caroline, Wynn."

And swallowing became a herculean chore again, as the lady wrapped the single syllable of his name in a low, husky contralto that conjured more of those sinful musings no respectable gentleman had a place having.

Reluctantly, he dropped his attention to her skirts she'd carefully arranged just above the tops of her knees.

Wynn cursed, and then lifted his gaze to hers. "I'm sorry."

"Oh, you needn't worry." Her lips twitched again in one of those hints of a grin, and he wondered what it would be to bring forth one of those complete smiles, wondered if it could captivate even more than reluctant ones. "I've several precocious siblings and nieces," she confided. "I'm hardly offended by—"

"I meant about your injury," he said quietly, recalling the reason for her flight out here. He lowered her skirts back into place. "I'm sorry I failed to catch you."

Her smile dipped. "Oh." She glanced over the top of his head, and he instantly wanted to call his apologies back, back to a place of that teasing smile. "It was hardly your fault." Her mouth tightened. "The fault belongs to my mother." With that, she hopped up, and then winced at the strain placed upon her knees.

Wynn jumped up beside her.

They lingered there, a moment more.

She should go.

He should leave.

They both should.

Not together.

And yet he was reluctant for the moment to end.

Caroline cleared her throat. "Thank you, Wynn."

He bowed his head. "Caroline."

The lady gathered up her pale-blue satin skirts, a shade put to shame by the bright hue of her eyes and lingered a moment more before turning on her heel, and marching off.

Wynn followed her movements the rest of the way, all the way, until she gripped the door handle and let herself inside. And his gaze remained locked on her through the leaded windowpane, as she walked the length of that corridor before disappearing from sight.

He glanced down at the damp kerchief in his hands, and then slowly tucked it inside the front of his jacket.

CHAPTER 7

LORD AND LADY CRAWFORD'S BALL had the distinction of being one of the most humiliating moments of Caroline's life.

It had also been the most magical.

It had been the same kind of magical that kept a lady from sleep, as she fought its hold, and struggled to cling to the moment that she'd wished to hold onto forever, that left one with a dreamy smile as one finally relinquished the fight and surrendered to a happy slumber. It left a lady lying in her bed the following morn, thinking of it still.

He'd raised her skirts and touched her leg.

Snuggling deeper into the warm sheets, Caroline dragged the coverlet up to her chin and closed her eyes… and her breath quickened.

He'd handled that limb with tenderness and warmth in his long-fingered, powerful hands.

And he'd also granted her the use of his first name.

Not, Lady Caroline and Lord Wynnchester.

But rather, simply *Wynn*.

And he'd spoken her name aloud, too, laying claim to it like one who'd been testing the sound of it on his lips.

It was her given name, and yet no gentleman beyond her brothers and male kin had ever uttered it.

And she'd begun to accept that none ever would.

Until him.

A dreamy sigh slipped out.

It surely spoke to how pitiable she, in fact, was that she'd been and remained enrapt at the feel of his hand upon her leg. This man who'd courted her sister, and who would have married Lettie had another gentleman not swept in before him.

Literally, right before him. As in the same morning of the same day.

And just like that, the bubble of hazy contentment burst like a proverbial balloon she'd once seen at a demonstration her sister Lettie had dragged her to years earlier.

For her mind, sluggish still from sleep and her musings, had also conveniently allowed Caroline to blot out the very reason he'd been at a knee, with her skirts up, in the first place.

The fall.

Only, he'd been so very gracious. He'd not shamed her or mocked her or even given her the cut direct as all society had after her first fall from grace. Oh, he easily *could* have. Instead, he'd sought her out to make sure she was unhurt, and when he'd gathered she was in fact hurt, had cared for her so tenderly. And the ease with which he'd spoken with her had been so very entrancing for a lady so accustomed to being either invisible or the object of gossip and mockery. He was…

With a groan, Caroline slunk lower onto the mattress and tugged the blankets firmly overhead.

To Marry Her Marquess

Courting another woman was what he was doing.

Wynn Masterson, the Earl of Exmoor, may be polite enough that he'd speak even to her, but he was not a gentleman who'd ever court one such as her.

She'd do well to remember that.

"Lady Caroline?" her maid, Agatha, called over concernedly.

"I need to…" *Run. Escape.* "…ready for the day, Agatha," she said from her position hidden under the blankets. And to her faithful maid's credit, she revealed no outward surprise at Caroline's speaking to her from under the blankets. As if it were the most natural thing in the world for Caroline to be hiding so.

Which, in fairness, it was.

There'd been plenty of times she'd wished to—and had—hidden herself away.

It had, however, been years. Many, many years.

She'd also discovered hiding changed nothing. "Have the papers arrived?" she asked; already knowing they had. Already knowing what was still being written about.

And even hidden as she was, she heard the hesitation; felt it. "They have, Lady Caroline."

Do not ask.

Do not ask.

I don't want to know.

Not truly, and not at all.

And yet, not knowing would also not make it go away—the gossip.

"And…was there any mention of…"

"Yes, my lady." The girl's voice emerged strained.

Caroline's stomach sank, and she wanted to remain hidden from the world, tucked away under the covers, and the world forever. One thing she was not, however, was a coward.

Slowly, she inched herself up and lowered the fabric a fraction. "What precisely are the papers saying?"

Her maid's rounded cheeks filled with color, and her dainty chin quivered, along with her full lower lip. Agatha gave her head a shake even as tears welled.

And Caroline's heart joined a place in her stomach. "Agatha," she gently prodded, sitting up in her bed.

"They are saying scandalous things about you *again*. Calling it shameful. A wanton…once m-more. D-D…" The girl clamped her wildly trembling lips shut and gave her head a forceful shake.

"Agatha," she repeated for a third time.

"Desperate," her maid whispered, and then promptly burst into tears, and…well…Caroline really wished to join her. Really, truly, desperately did.

Closing her eyes, Caroline let herself fall back into the mattress, bouncing slightly as the feathered bedding dipped under her movement. She dragged a pillow over her head.

How long would it take a person to suffocate oneself?

Mayhap she was more a coward than she credited after all.

Alas…

Gasping for breath, she wrenched the pillow from her face. Her chest heaved from the sudden influx of air into her lungs and the agonizing humiliation of being talked about so. *Again.*

Once more, she was the lady everyone would be speaking about. She, who had managed to remain as visible as the painted wallpaper along the sides of ballrooms these past years.

She'd never appreciated just how glorious the ignominy

she'd achieved was until she'd lost it.

This time, unlike last, she'd not lost it for all the worst reasons. This time, it was through no fault of her own.

Even so, they'd mock her the same way, laugh at her, call her—

Caroline froze, recalling the word that had set Agatha weeping.

Desperate.

She slapped her palms over her face. Somehow that was worse than all the meanest, ugliest things they'd said of her before. Caroline dragged the blankets overhead a second time.

"*No*, Lady Caroline," her maid pleaded. "You mustn't do that."

Hide? Absolutely she must and should.

Because everyone was gossiping about her. Every—

Caroline went absolutely still.

Everyone.

Her heart thudded, sickeningly dull inside her chest.

That everyone would include her mother.

"I have to go." Caroline swung her legs over the side of the bed, and then immediately regretted that sudden movement as her injured knees screamed in protest. Not even that pain, however, could keep her from self-preservation. "Immediately."

Out of this room. Out of this household.

For it was a certainty the dowager marchioness was coming.

"Of course, Lady Caroline." Seemingly restored by those no-nonsense, direct orders, and finding grounding in that purpose given her by her mistress, Agatha stopped weeping and sprinted over to the robin's egg blue painted oak armoire.

A short while later, the girl had Caroline readied to face the day or at least, run away from it—delay the inevitable meeting and all. As her faithful maid rushed off to have the carriage readied for them, Caroline ducked her head outside her rooms. She peeked left and then right down the wide corridors.

Empty.

Hastening from her chambers, she drew the door shut quietly behind her, then started for the foyer.

She reached the end of the hall and peered around the curve—and then promptly drew back.

Her stomach churned in protest.

Bloody hell. She silently screamed that curse she'd not dragged out since she'd been a naïve lady rushing about to steal away with Dylan.

It had been inevitable.

One did not simply escape the Dowager Marchioness of Guilford's machinations without finding oneself in that obstinate lady's crosshairs.

It had been a wonder Caroline had avoided this meeting as long as she had; that she hadn't followed Caroline to her rooms last evening.

Though in fairness, her mother *had* sought her out; rattling the locked door, until Miles had come and ordered her away from Caroline's chambers.

Which would have only leant to her mother's rage.

One could not stay behind a locked door forever.

That was a locked door that one did not own.

"Caroline Rose Brookfield, would you stop hiding around corners like a child."

Caroline Rose Brookfield. Her mother had not used the three-name summons since Caroline's public disgrace all those years ago. And she found her adult self, wanting to race from those chilling tones the very same way naïve-Caroline of years past had.

Yes, there'd only been so long she could hide.

Swallowing a sigh, Caroline stepped from behind the corner.

Her mother stood with her arms folded and a newspaper clutched awkwardly in her beginning-to-wrinkle hands.

Caroline inclined her head. "Mother," she greeted. "Good morning." And with that slight bow of her head, she changed direction, heading the opposite way.

"Good morning!" her mother squawked. "Good morning?" And then, in a clear sign of the dowager marchioness's outrage and upset, she sprinted down the hall to join Caroline. "*That* is all you'll say?" she demanded when she'd reached Caroline's side.

"What else is there to say?" Caroline gritted out, increasing her stride and earning a gasp from her last living parent.

"Caroline Rose Brookfield, have a care with your pace. Young ladies do not go running about."

They did when they were running from something. Or in this case, *someone*.

"How could you have done this to us?" her mother bemoaned, as she walked at her brisk clip, clinging to Caroline's side like tenacious ivy.

Caroline stopped abruptly at the corner leading to the breakfast room. "How could *I* have done this? How could *I*?" she repeated that question at a slightly slower, and more emphasized uptilt to that query. The mistake she'd made with Dylan had been entirely her fault. But this? This time Caroline was certainly not to blame. "How could *you* have done this?

Her mother drew back, touching an affronted hand to her breast. "Surely you are not suggesting... you are not implying I'm the one who is to blame for what happened with Lord Exmoor?"

"You shoved me at the gentleman, Mother." And she felt her cheeks go warm as she recalled the footmen stationed outside the breakfast room, certainly close enough for them to hear that bald statement. Caroline dropped her voice to a frantic whisper. "You actually *threw* me at him."

Her mother, however, showed no such awareness of the servants close by. To her they were and had always been invisible. "Of course, I did. Just as I did with your sister, but she had the good sense to fall gracefully and not flat on her face, Caroline," her mother snapped.

Yes, but then that had been because the marquess had likely wanted to catch her, whereas Caroline...Caroline couldn't—then and now—have begged a gentleman into spitting on her if her skirts had caught fire.

Only that isn't at all true, a voice whispered, equally taunting her and tempting her with the reminder of her skirts rucked up about her knees as he'd gently tended her inj—

"What have you done?" her mother bemoaned, snapping Caroline to the moment, and she gave thanks her mother would only ever construe that blush as a humiliated one, and not one elicited by wicked thoughts about Wynn's hands upon her.

"It was one thing when no one was talking about you, but now everyone is and for all the wrong reasons again."

Unable to form a suitable defense of herself because there was none, Caroline bit the inside of her cheek.

And then, salvation came.

"Aunt Caroline!"

She and her mother looked over as Faith and Violet came rushing down the hall.

"We have been looking for you," Faith said, when they reached her. "Grandmother." Her niece's belated greeting was not lost on Caroline. "The carriage is readied."

Caroline furrowed her brow.

"The carriage is readied?" The dowager passed a glance between her granddaughters and Caroline. "Readied for what?"

Faith gave Caroline a pointed look. "For the hothouse. Violet and I had asked Aunt Caroline to accompany us, as Violet's…governess, Miss Wilson, is beginning lessons on…on…"

Then it hit her. They were trying to save Caroline from her mother. "Floral arrangements," Caroline blurted. "Miss Wilson intends to begin—"

"Lessons," Faith interjected.

Violet groaned. "She is?" The younger girl caught the sideways glance Faith shot her. "I meant, she is!" she exclaimed. "Huzzah." Violet held her arms aloft and pumped them like a rider who'd just won the Queen Anne Stakes.

Caroline's mother found her voice. "You do not need Caroline. The governess can—"

"Oh, no," Faith and Violet spoke in unison. "It *must* be Aunt Caroline."

The dowager marchioness proved no match for the whirlwind that was the younger girls, as they hurriedly inserted themselves between mother and daughter. Catching Caroline by the arms, they steered her from the townhouse to the waiting carriage.

The moment they'd scrambled inside, the driver shut

the door quickly behind them.

Drawing a deep breath, Caroline sank back in the folds of the bench.

She was free.

For now.

CHAPTER 8

THE MORNING FOLLOWING THE DUKE and Duchess of Crawford's ball, Wynn sat breaking his fast with his sisters.

Breakfast was always a noisy affair in the Masterson household.

With the addition of Wynn's closest friend, the Earl of Denbigh, at this particular meal, it proved even more so.

Though, in fairness, all events in the Masterson household proved to be boisterous.

"I, for one, feel bad for the lady," his youngest sister, Elspeth declared from behind the gossip sheet she held in one hand. "No lady should be so shamed," she declared, her gaze still on the pages.

"No lady should be reading a newspaper in the middle of a meal, and yet here we are," Denbigh drawled.

Elspeth popped her head around her pages. "We're not in the middle of the meal. We're at the end of it." She gestured to the nearly empty plates around the table. She stuck her tongue out at Denbigh who returned the gesture in kind.

If ever a day called for a chocolate biscuit, this was the one. Wynn reached for it.

Alice shot a hand out, grabbing for the confectionary treat—and winning it—by a fraction of a second.

"You don't deserve the chocolate biscuit," she chided.

"Et tu, Brutus?" Denbigh said dryly, with all the loyalty only a best chum was capable of.

Both Wynn's sisters glared at the earl in return, and reflexively the suddenly sheepish fellow drew his plate close, protecting his own as-of-yet untouched biscuit.

"A chocolate biscuit belongs to one who does things like rescue a lady from ruin and scandal," Alice said, relieving Wynn of his dessert.

He tensed.

Elspeth lent a nod of support to her elder sister's pronouncement.

Wynn felt heat creep up his neck. No, having failed so spectacularly to both protect Alice from a predatory gentleman and catch Caroline when she fell the evening prior, the last thing he deserved was any kind of sweet treat.

"Hey, now," Denbigh said, with the same loyalty he'd shown since their Eton days. "Place blame where blame is due. With the mother who continues to fling her daughters at poor Exmoor. Your brother is hardly to blame." With that, he snatched the treat from Alice's fingers just as she had it at her mouth.

Sputtering with outrage, she attempted to grab it back.

Holding the biscuit out of her reach, the earl took a large bite of the treat and winked.

Alice clucked her tongue. "It is in bad form."

"Indeed, it is. Stealing biscuits from a lady," Elspeth muttered; still tender enough in her fourteen years and unaware of their sister's scandal to believe there was no greater offense than that.

From around a mouthful of dessert, Denbigh only widened his smile, earning an eye-roll from Wynn's siblings.

Alice knocked a fist on the table. "I'm not talking about Denbigh's biscuit thievery. I'm speaking about Wynn's failure to catch Lady Caroline."

Yes, he'd failed spectacularly, indeed. In so many ways.

"He did not fail," Denbigh protested.

Wynn's sisters responded in unison, "He did."

"He certainly did."

While they debated, Wynn's stomach knotted. He might not be to blame, but neither had he helped. The memory of her as she'd been on that terrace, her knees smarting.

And then a different image slipped in, a forbidden one.

Of Caroline Brookfield with her skirts in hand, and that satin fabric rucked high about her legs, exposing long, lithe, graceful limbs.

Limbs he'd had in his hands.

Desire roared to life as potent and powerful as it had been last evening.

And yet as appealing as she'd been with her skirts around her knees, he'd no place thinking of her. Because there was Lady Beatrice.

Lady Beatrice, whom he intended to begin courting. Why did the thought of that not bring the same relief it had before the incident with Lady Caroline?

"I for one feel bad the lady is saddled with a mother as mercenary as that one," Denbigh declared, interrupting Wynn's thinking.

His sisters each thumped the table with a fist. "Here, here," they concurred.

At last, they'd landed on a point they could all agree on.

"What are we discussing?"

The occupants of the room collectively looked up and over as the marchioness sailed into the room.

Wynn resisted an urge to groan.

"We're talking about how Exmoor failed Lady Caroline last evening," Alice supplied.

With a frown, his mother joined them at the table. "He most certainly did not. The lady's mother failed her. That mama is a scandal."

Yes, she was. What it must be for the lady to have one such as that for a mother.

"You really should have caught her," his sister Elspeth, this time, chided.

Wynn resisted the need to groan. "I know. *I know*," he repeated.

"He caught the other one, and look what that got him," Denbigh pointed out; earning a laugh from Wynn's youngest sister, and matching dark looks from Wynn and his mother.

The earl had the good grace to slump in his dining chair. Sheepishly, he held his palms up.

The marchioness drew in a deep breath. "We have a problem," she spoke with such an unexpected-for-her somberness, it penetrated the usual playfulness of her children present, and everyone went quiet.

Wynn stiffened.

Alice paled.

Their mother set a newspaper down on the table. "Have you seen this?"

Elspeth, wholly unaware of the tension emanating from her other siblings, popped up in her chair. "We've not seen anything. When we'd begun discussing Lady

Caroline and Wynn's failure to catch her, he banished all papers." The girl reached for the pages, but her mother held them back.

"This isn't about Lady Caroline," she said in more of that somber seriousness, and fear knocked away harder in his chest.

Oh God, it was about Alice. Someone had deduced something. Surely his mother didn't intend to have this discussion—

"This is about Wynn," his mother said, setting the paper down beside her.

The moment she did, Elspeth grabbed it with greedy fingers, and her eyes flew across the page as she devoured whatever words were written there.

It was not about Alice, or speculation about her near-faint last evening. It was a moment of such profound relief for Wynn that it was an even longer moment before he registered just what his mother had said.

"*Me?*" he echoed. What in blazes were they saying about him now?

"Look here," Elspeth said excitedly, jabbing at the pages, she proceeded to read. "Whispers and stories and tales and legends once swirled about a necklace proffered by a Romany peddler, of a talisman that was purported to earn the lady a heart of a duke."

Denbigh burst out laughing. "Of course, there's such a legend," he said around his fit of amusement.

Elspeth paused in her reading to glare at the earl. "May I finish?" There was a warning there.

One that even with her more tender years, Denbigh, who'd spent enough time in this household alongside Wynn, knew meant to don a more serious set to his expression or risk the wrath of a Masterson child.

"My apologies," he demurred. "Please do continue."

Ensured the room's attention was on her once more, Elspeth gave those pages a snap, cleared her throat, and resumed her reading.

"At various points, throughout various seasons, such necklace has been seen on the necks of different ladies. Many of whom went on to wed—a duke."

"Did *all* of them?" Wynn muttered. "It's not like London is crawling with young, eligible dukes."

"But here is the interesting part." Elspeth spoke excitedly.

"Really?" Alice asked. "Because I rather think there being a magical necklace that could earn a lady the heart of a duke is probably the most fascinating part." She gave her younger sister's curl a playful tug.

"And here I'd never taken you as so mercenary as to be intent on a dukedom," Denbigh said to Alice, following it with a wink.

She wrinkled her nose.

The marchioness clapped her hands. "Hush." She looked to her youngest daughter. "Go on."

"They say a new legend has been born of the tale." Elspeth spoke in quiet, mysterious way meant to ensure the room's interest.

The room, which did not disappoint.

Even Wynn found himself hanging on.

"The legend involves none other than the distinguished, eminently respectable Marquess of E..." With that his sister lowered her pages, and all eyes went to Wynn.

Wynn, who was waiting to hear what the gossips were saying about him and was also still attempting to process whom the poor Marquess of E who was the source of this latest legend.

He'd been the Earl of Astor for so long and only just recently the claimant of that new title, before belatedly realizing...the papers were speaking of him.

"Me?" he blurted. Oh, bloody hell.

"None other." Alice smiled widely at the table that had gone silent. "And you were all worried that women wouldn't want to marry Wynn. Now he's going to be flooded by interested ladies."

"Flooded by ladies interested in earning the affections of another man. Do give me that," the marchioness muttered and plucked the pages from her fingers. She proceeded to read, her eyes frantically skimming the pages, her mouth moving silently as she read back the words that had already been read before her gaze ultimately landed upon the place where Elspeth had left off. Worry filled her eyes. "This will not do," she lamented. "This will not do at all." Raising her voice, she read aloud from those pages. "The new legend purports that any lady who is courted by the Marquess of E will find herself married, and not to the pitiable..."

"Pitiable," he mouthed.

"But eminently respectable," she carried on.

"Eminently respectable. There you go, chum. That's better," Denbigh volunteered.

"Marquess of E."

The marchioness let the pages drop. "My child... cursed."

It took a moment for that to register. Surely his mother was not suggesting...she was not saying...

"You don't believe that rubbish?" he asked incredulously. Except he knew the truth.

"That every lady you court will one day fall for another, and a duke?" his mother scoffed. "Hardly. As you've already cleverly pointed out, there's not a limitless number of dukes running about the Ton. Though, it does certainly seem as if there is an endless supply of those young, dashing gentlemen." She added that part more quietly as if speaking to herself.

Since his father's untimely and unexpected death, his mother had taken to visiting a mysterious woman who read of some equally mysterious cards and continually came back with predictions and prophecies. Ultimately, however, all questions and concerns came back to Wynn and his lack of a wife.

"You...unwanted and unmarried?" His mother dabbed at the corners of her eyes. "It is not to be born. First, he was thrown over by the now-Duchess of Crawford...and then Lady Lettie."

He gritted his teeth. "That was a lifetime ago." *Furthermore...* "And I was not attempting to wed Lady Daisy. I was attempting to court her." At the insistence of the Duke of Crawford who in a perverse, peculiar show had ordered him gone and then married the lady himself.

"It's because he's cursed," Elspeth piped in.

Exasperated, Wynn through his hands up. "I'm not cursed."

"Aren't you?" she asked. "Aren't you?" she pressed him a second time, overemphasizing those two syllables; somehow managing to make them five. "You are very much like Papa." Sadness filled Elspeth's eyes. "And he was cursed, too."

"Father was not cursed," Alice said sharply.

A devoted father, oft visiting his children in the nurseries and riding with both his son and daughters—a match between the affectionate marquess and Wynn's devoted mother had been a pairing that defied most of the cold, empty unions of the Ton.

"He died young," Alice said softly. "Choking on an olive pit."

The room fell quiet with even Denbigh suitably quiet at the reminder of the late Marquess of Exmoor. A devoted, more jovial family man there hadn't been.

"Yes, that is right," the marchioness said into the quiet. "Your father died young. It was nothing more than a sudden accident, which should serve as a reminder to you of just how precarious life and our circumstances are." She spoke that last part more to herself.

As soon as the words left her mouth, she and Alice both paled.

"What are our circumstances?" Elspeth asked the room at large. "What are our circumstances?" she repeated when no one made to answer.

"I'm courting Lady Beatrice," Wynn blurted into the quiet.

Every pair of eyes swung his way.

Unnerved at being the subject of anyone's notice, even his own family's, Wynn cleared his throat. "The circumstances mother is referring to is me, and the fact that I'm a thirty-five-year-old marquess long overdue to wed."

Alice stared at him with accusatory eyes. "Lady Beatrice?"

"Lady Beatrice?" his mother whispered, that name a blend of reverence and joy.

"The idea came to me last evening," he said. "She is respectable and lovely and would make me a suitable match."

A frown formed on Alice's lips. "A *suitable* match? How very romantic."

What in blazes did she expect of him? But then, she

was a romantic. Her idealism was what ultimately led to her ruin.

Their mother, however, ignored that palpable displeasure. "Why, yes. Yes, Lady Beatrice would make you a perfect bride." And for the first time in longer than he could remember, a very real smile formed on her lips.

Yes, she would. So why then did he not feel the same eagerness to begin courting the lady that he had last evening? Before Lady Caroline and their talk, and…that touch. Unnerved, Wynn shoved back his chair and stood. "If you'll excuse me? I intend to pay the lady a call."

"Flowers," his mother interrupted. "Might I suggest you show up to your visit with flowers. All ladies love flowers."

"He got Lady Lettie flowers, for all the good it did—*oww*," Elspeth winced at the slight pinch their mother gave.

Yes, he had gotten Lady Lettie flowers, and ultimately, she'd chosen another.

Time was running out for Alice and all the Masterson family.

This courtship, unlike the prior two, could not end in anything but marriage.

CHAPTER 9

Following her unexpected exchange with Wynn last evening, Caroline had begun to see him everywhere. As her nieces followed Violet's governess among the blossoms at Palmers Garden Centres, Caroline lingered amidst her dreams.

In her mind, the air still crackled, and her body still tingled as she recalled the very moment he'd knelt beside her, and sought permission, before tenderly guiding her dress up to look after her smarting leg.

And from the moment he'd touched his long, powerful fingers to that exposed flesh, she'd ceased to feel either pain or the chill of the rainy night air. All coherent, ordered thoughts had fled her mind, and she'd been left with a mix of both feeling and disjointed musings that ultimately all went back to the dashing marquess.

She'd lost her virtue to a scoundrel; never in all the quick interludes they'd stolen together had she felt any of the heat or longing she'd known with Wynn's sure touch.

It was also why, after their meeting on the terrace, she

was seeing him everywhere—including, here now at the garden centres.

And yet…

Poised at the back of the hothouse among the carnations—that flower that signified fascination—Caroline followed him with her gaze, as he moved purposefully throughout the shop.

No. He was very much real and very much here now.

Wynn paused occasionally beside a flower, continuing on from each. The forget-me-nots. The pansies.

Caroline's breath caught.

It was very foreign to find a gentleman who put such effort—to put any effort—into picking out flowers for his lady.

In all the time she'd been coming to Palmers Garden Centres, she had learned that most gentlemen sent servants to see to the chore on their behalf. The rare few that did come hastily grabbed whichever bouquet the shopkeeper thrust his way.

And then there was Wynn Masterson, the Marquess of Exmoor, who came himself, by himself, and saw to the task himself.

Only, with the way he perused the shop, it didn't seem like very much a chore at all.

Nor was it the first time Caroline had seen Wynn here.

It was, however, the first time she'd seen him since her sister had ended her courtship with the gentleman.

And it was a certainty that this particular bouquet would be of a romantic nature, that those blooms he now studiously considered were for a sweetheart.

From where she stood behind a table of hibiscus, Caroline pressed a hand over her wildly thumping heart.

He is considering which flowers to give a young lady. One

who was *not* Caroline's sister.

The same memory that had robbed her of sleep, and only for wonderful reasons, filled her head now, and Caroline closed her eyes, each moment from last evening, playing out in bright beautiful color, like that kaleidoscope her nephew, Miles and Philippa's adopted son Paddy was forever playing with.

"I…would you allow me to see to your injury… A wise woman once pointed out how ridiculous it is we are forbidden from talking about the human body as we all have one… Wynn…That is, given this evening using our Christian names seems more appropriate."

Caroline's eyes fluttered open.

Stop.

I must get control of myself.

I am not a young, simpering debutante. Not anymore. I'm a grown woman…

She was also a grown woman who'd accepted that no good, honorable gentleman would ever court her. Until now.

For there was Wynn.

Caroline stole another peek at the gentleman.

He lifted his head, and his gaze collided with hers.

All thoughts fled Caroline's head and her heart kicked up a funny beat. That same funny beat it had last evening when he'd examined her leg.

His eyes were a shade of blue the likes of which she'd never before seen. Some odd blending of blues and greens and even some violets. It was an odd color, and also certainly the only reason she noted them. Because she certainly had no place noticing.

That reminder blared loudly in her mind, but still, she remained hopeless to look away.

He inclined his head in a bashful way.

Was his a polite acknowledgment? Or a greeting? Or was he merely shy at having been discovered here by her? That only further endeared him to her.

Caroline bowed hers in return before glancing down at the daffodils.

How many times had she noted him throughout the Season, at various Ton affairs, or during one of his visits to her sister? So many. Every time he'd come to call on Lettie, Caroline had secretly, shamefully, relished the brief exchanges she'd shared with him.

She felt his approach before she saw him.

"Caroline," he greeted warmly.

Caroline looked up.

"Wynn," she murmured, sinking into a curtsy. At seven inches past five feet Caroline was taller than most men… the marquess proved one of the rare exceptions. An inch or two past six feet, he was tall by his own right, but not so very tall that she had to crane her neck. It was another detail she'd no place noting, and silently reassured herself the observation came from the fact that during her years as a shunned wallflower, she'd also become somewhat adept at noting details that escaped most other people.

"Do you have a preference?"

He'd been wavering between the forget-me-nots and pansies.

He'd been considering both flowers for the better part of five minutes now; vacillating back and forth from one to the other.

They were both disastrous choices.

That was if one's selection was of a romantic nature.

Then the significance of what he was asking, hit her.

Her mind and soul screamed and rejoiced silently

together.

A preference? She'd have taken a weed wrapped with a ribbon, just so she might claim she'd received a bouquet, just once in her life. Not even Dylan, the scoundrel who'd charmed her and then sought to marry her for her dowry—before running off when it was apparent he'd not have what he'd truly wished—had brought her flowers.

Caroline shook her head dumbly, attempting to find her way in this exchange. "I…"

She was rubbish at discourse. Not witty. Not charming. Not breezy or light. Not anymore. Where her sisters and brothers were capable of brevity, she'd become capable of only freezing when eyes were trained on her. And yet, the marquess intended to court her, still.

Instead of being deterred by her tongue-tied state, Wynn studied the nearby flowers with a contemplative expression. The level of thought left his high, broad brow creased, and his hard, square chin firmed.

He was going with the forget-me-nots.

She knew it by the way his eyes lingered upon the white and pale blue blooms.

And why should he not? They sounded romantic in name.

"They are a disastrous choice," she blurted, and Wynn stopped, and slowly turned back.

His dark brows came together in a single line. "Beg pardon?"

Her stomach dropped. She'd offended him. Of course, she had. That was to be expected of a young woman absolutely unskilled and unpracticed in the ways of conversing with gentlemen. Or really anyone. Aside from her younger nieces who'd become like de facto sisters, there weren't even lady friends where she was concerned.

Not anymore.

Caroline cleared her throat. "It is just...I believe there might be..." she amended, "...a better choice."

His brow creased again in an endearing way as he studied the flowers he'd been about to purchase before her interruption. There was a boy-like quality to that puzzlement, a hesitancy from a powerful gentleman with aquiline features and slightly hawk-like nose. At last, he lifted his head, and Caroline made herself stop her search of his features and prayed he'd attribute her hot, blushing cheeks to the warmth of the greenhouse.

His eyes locked with hers, and it was as though that piercing, powerful gaze slid slowly over her face before lingering once more on her eyes, then stilled. "They... are lovely," he murmured, and her *heart* stilled, and then picked up a wild cadence, even as her breath froze.

He frowned and dipped his gaze down. "Or rather, I thought they were," he muttered, more to himself, and even those flowers.

"Oh, no. They are a perfectly lovely flower. Most beautiful," she said, and he shifted his focus back Caroline's way. "It is just..."

He stared at her.

Not in the awkward, uncomfortable way of those who still recalled her scandal from long ago but rather patiently. Nay, more than that. Curiously.

He appeared curious.

"It is just that...there is a whole language around flowers."

"Indeed?" He sounded genuinely intrigued...and by something she'd said.

She nodded. "Each bud has a different meaning, and the meaning behind those," she pointed to the flowers he'd been considering, "isn't romantic."

A wistful little grin hovered at his lips. And goodness that quirk of his mouth proved as dangerous to the rhythm of her heartbeat as the intensity of the blue eyes he'd trained on her before. And then softly he said,

"Nor can I find, amid my lonely walk,
By rivulet, or spring, or wet road-side,
That blue and bright-eyed floweret of the brook,
Hope's gentle gem, the sweet Forget-me-not!"

Her breath caught, and this time, she did not try to fight it.

This time, she did not seek to still the slight, noticeable intake of her breath as he recited those mesmerizing words of—who? Whose words were those? They were familiar.

"Coleridge," he said, as if he'd known the question in her mind.

"Coleridge," she whispered back that name in an echo.

Wynn was reciting poetry to her, and it was heady stuff. Powerful and as potent and entrancing as the look he'd trained upon her, moments ago when she'd thought he was entranced by her eyes.

"The fellow can't be wrong," he said without inflection.

"Actually, he is," she said. "Most people don't know it." Why was it so very easy speaking with this man?

"But you do." There was a slight teasing quality, a familiarity to his words, and her pulse raced all the faster.

Never could she have imagined she'd be here, with this man.

"Its official name is myosotis, which means mouse toe," she explained, and even as she said it, realized he likely knew, because a gentleman like him would have taken enough Latin courses over his life to know that definition. "Because of the shape of the leaves." She motioned to the flower, and he followed the tip of her index finger that now pointed at the stems in his right hand. "But that is not all."

"No?" he asked, sounding curiously intrigued, which was an unfamiliar sentiment for Caroline to enlist in any man, and it proved as heady as the poem she'd thought he recited to her.

She shook her head. "There is an old legend, a tale of a German knight who'd been at a stream, collecting forget-me-nots for his lady. He lost his footing while picking them, and the swift current carried him off, and as he did, he was said to have cried out, 'Forget-me-not.'"

Wynn stared wide-eyed at her.

No man had ever gone wide-eyed over anything she'd said, for the simple reason being, she'd never strung together this many sentences for a gentleman since before she'd been ruined. In fact, she'd not believed herself capable of such a feat any longer, and she felt herself... warming to speaking. And speaking to him.

"Then there is, of course, the fact King Henry VIII had the emblem of the forget-me-not sewn onto the fronts of all his robes." Her mouth pulled. "Given the history of his treatment of his many wives, one would be hard-pressed to want any flower with *that* remembrance attached to it."

Wynn froze, and Caroline did as well that she'd said as much. Horror held her motionless.

And then, the marquess tossed his head back and roared with laughter.

Caroline started, and then it occurred to her that he wasn't laughing at her, but rather at the words she'd spoken, and it pulled a laugh from her; and then they were laughing together.

When his laughter abated, the marquess gave his head a shake. "Yes, I daresay those are all solid reasons to avoid this flower," he said, and as if on cue, a shopkeeper came and collected that bouquet, carrying it off, and leaving him with—

"What of these?" Wynn asked, holding aloft the collection of vibrant purple pansies gathered in a lovely pink ribbon.

A bow such as that one she'd keep forever. She'd wind it in her hair, loop it over her wrist, sleep with it under her pillow. Though, any bow he selected she'd have cherished in a like way.

The ghost of a grin teased at his beautifully firm, hard mouth. "Pansies for your thoughts," he murmured, that most famous line of Ophelia, about the flowers.

A wistful smile pulled her lips up in the corners. "Kiss-me-quick," she murmured, and the marquess stilled. "That is the alternate name for them," she explained on a rush, certain her cheeks were destined to set fire this day. *Oh, blast.* "Not that I was suggesting. Not that I would be so inappropriate as to…" Except she'd once been so inappropriate.

Wynn chuckled. "No, of course not." From someone else, from anyone else, from everyone else before him, that laugh would have been derisive and cold. "I would never dare think as much, Caroline."

She searched his face for a hint of disapproval or disgust. That was not there.

His laugh was not mocking, but still, it caused an odd tightness in her chest that he should find amusement in the fact that she would never be inappropriate. Because even though it was a certainty as factual as rain in England, she despised that she was so very staid and predictable and uninteresting to the world.

"Given that romantic name, I should say it would be perfect."

"Oh, yes, they are perfectly lovely," Caroline murmured.

"But by your tone, they are not suitable."

By her tone? She had a tone? That was, a tone that someone—that he—recognized? Her heart missed yet another beat that day. "Well, it is just that it all depends on when they were picked."

Wynn came over, joining her at the side of the table she occupied, and her breath caught a funny way at his nearness. "This I must hear," he murmured.

"The legend holds that if you pick one and it has dew upon it, it will cause the death of a loved one."

He moved his gaze over her face, and there was almost a reverent awe in the way he touched his eyes upon each feature. "You know a good deal about flowers."

"When a lady lands herself in a scandal, she also finds an endless amount of time to herself."

As soon as the words left her, she wanted to call them back. Why had she reminded him of her past sins? Only, he didn't turn away in disgust. Instead, he drifted closer. "What happened?" he asked quietly. And then it hit her.

He didn't know the details. Somehow, he remained the one person in London who'd not gathered the whole sordid story of her ruin and the reason for her subsequent ostracization. Of course. It was why he'd not disdained her, and why he'd thought of courting her.

Now, she'd go and kill whatever affection had bloomed between them.

And she proved a coward, not wanting to breathe the words aloud that would send him running. Reflexively, she shook her head slightly, looking away.

She felt Wynn move. Felt his nearness. Her body strangely in tune with his movements in a way it had not been before. *Never.*

Then, ever so softly, she felt the fleeting brush of Wynn's fingers against hers. It was a tender, discreet caress; so very private, and all the more intimate for the stolen quality to it.

Heart hammering, Caroline looked up.

Do not tell him... a voice in her mind screamed. And yet, she couldn't *not* tell him. He deserved to know.

Unnerved, unable to look at him anymore, she drifted deeper down the aisle, moving away from the center of the shop, and towards the pale white lilies. "I was young. Innocent." But then, all debutantes were young and innocent. Not all of them made the manner of grave mistakes that Caroline had. "He was so very charming. He'd always have a clever quip and would tell jests that made me laugh." But never talking to her about anything truly meaningful; not about life or love. "It was new and wonderful and felt so very exciting."

She stared blankly at the flowers before her; absently she stretched a fingertip out, and ever so delicately brushed a finger along the satiny soft petal. "But he did not truly wish to marry me. Not for anything but my fortune, that is."

Even all these years later, bitterness still echoed in her voice. Not with regret at having been so rejected, but rather because she'd been so foolish as to give herself to such a man.

"Afterwards," she explained, "my family and I retired

to the country. For a long while there were no balls or… or any events. There was just time that was my own. It was too hard being around my family. After what I'd done, I couldn't look at them for the longest time, and so I grabbed books and went to where no one was."

"And where was that?" he asked softly.

"The greenhouse. I would just sit there, amongst the flowers, while the gardener tended them. He didn't mind my scandal. And we would just talk, and he told me all these fascinating stories."

"About the meaning of flowers."

She nodded. "Exactly." Unnerved by all she'd shared, and the likely scorn that would inevitably come, Caroline stared out across the largely empty hothouse to the sea of bright, cheerful flowers around them. Her nieces who'd accompanied her plucked flowers, arranging them; absorbed in that task, giggling and laughing, both of them so very innocent. As Caroline had once been, too. Not much older than Faith was now when Caroline had made the most tragic of errors in judgment.

And then she felt it.

Wynn slipped his fingers through hers, twining them, conferring a silent, intimate support, and in that instant, she fell so very much in love with him.

She loved him for not running away. She loved him for not mocking her or rejecting her as all of society had.

"You were better off without him," he said quietly.

For a long while, she'd not been. Because there was no future for jilted brides. All of society had assumed she'd given him her virtue. Nor had they been wrong in those assumptions.

Caroline drew in a ragged breath. "Yes. I know that…" She lifted her eyes, meeting his gaze with her own.

"Now."

Something heated and powerful passed between them. Some silent emotion, a connection so strong and so deep, it kept the whole world at bay so that it was only she and he, locked in this moment and this place, and she wanted to remain here with him forever.

Suddenly, he drew his fingers back, and she silently wept at that loss.

He waved a hand about the greenhouse. "Are there any suitably romantic flowers that do not connote death or harm or hurt?" There was a playful quality to his voice.

"Oh, yes," she assured him. "Many." Caroline walked purposefully to the flowers in question, and he was joining her, and it felt natural. It felt so very comfortable and easy. "There are these," she said, pausing beside a table of daffodils. "The daffodil suggests a regard for someone. And these." She started over to the adjacent display of hot pink, blue, and purple blooms. "The morning glory denotes affection."

Wynn brought them to a stop alongside a different table. "What of this one?"

"Lavender," she murmured. It was the scent worn by her sister.

Caroline's teeth troubled at the flesh of her cheek. "Lavender is associated with distrust."

He stilled.

"Not that those who wear the fragrance of the flower are not to be trusted," she said on a rush. "Many women love the flower and the fragrance, and many are not at all distrustful and..." *Rambling.* Another first for her. "Anyway there is not even necessarily anything true—" He lifted his dark eyebrows—"about the flowers," she said quickly. "Not the people who wear the flowers." His lips twitched. "Not that people wear flowers." *Just stop talking.* "They wear the fragrance." And this time he didn't fight the smile. *Or mayhap it was that he couldn't stop from laughing at my yammering.* "But you of course know that. That people don't wear flowers," she finished lamely.

Except...

"Some people wear flowers," she felt inclined to point out. "Coronets. Blooms woven in their hair, and...and..." She blinked slowly. "What were we talking about?"

"I believe it began as something about the appropriateness of the lavender flower." His eyes twinkled.

She'd never known eyes could.

"I daresay there are enough options in flowers to avoid ones that have such a negative connotation."

"I wasn't suggesting that you shouldn't," she said softly. "If you feel they...evoke..." thoughts of her...something, then that something has far greater meaning than some superstition or tale about the flower."

"I'm grateful for the edification in flowers." And said in that serious way, he made her believe him. Not even her own brothers, who were most devoted, had taken time to inquire about her interest in flowers.

Her pulse pounded.

"Unless you would rather not," he said quietly.

Caroline cocked her head.

"Provide that edification," he supplanted.

Provide that edification?

Then his words, their meaning, and the hesitancy now with which he spoke, and which reflected in his eyes hit her.

"I would be happy to," she blurted.

Across the way, Faith paused in her study of some purple violets and looked up. Caroline's niece took in Caroline and Wynn conversing. Happy surprise lit the younger girl's eyes. And then, hastily, her niece yanked her focus back to Violet.

A slight flush marred Wynn's cheeks. "You are under no obligation to do so as I trust you have affairs of your own to attend," he said, misunderstanding the reason for her silence.

"No! I would be happy to." In fact, there was nowhere else she wished to be than here with him.

And so, with that, Caroline led Wynn throughout the shop, gesturing as she went, and explaining the significance associated with each flower. From the apple blossom on down to the zinnia.

As they walked, he put questions to her about certain flowers: the aster, delphinium, globe thistle, and poppy.

And as he did, she learned his interest in those specific blooms hinted at his preference for the color blue.

At last, they completed their circle about the shop, coming to a halt beside the place where it began.

The forget-me-nots.

"I am in awe of the depth and breadth of your knowledge of flowers, my lady." Wynn's gaze locked with hers. "I cannot thank you enough."

"It was my pleasure," she said softly. And it had been.

He lingered a moment more, his gaze also lingering on her face, and time stood still.

The earth ceased to move.

"I found them, Aunt Caroline!"

They both jumped, brought crashing jarringly back to the moment by the arrival of Caroline's niece, Violet.

Barreling past Faith, who struggled to keep up, the young girl carried a basket filled to overflowing of fuchsia-colored cylindrical corms with sword-shaped stems bare of leaves.

"Your favorite," the girl said, turning the basket over to Caroline's care as if she'd not interrupted—anything, at all. "Oh," she said, as if only just noticing her aunt had company.

Slightly breathless, Faith reached her younger sister. "Hullo, Aunt Caroline." There was an apology in her voice. One that indicated she'd caught the undercurrents of Caroline's meeting with the marquess and regretted being unable to stop Violet from interrupting.

"Hello, Faith." Caroline filled the brief moment of awkwardness with only more awkwardness. "Faith, Violet, you remember Lord Exmoor." She instantly wanted to call back that ridiculous reminder.

"As if I could forget." Violet spoke with a sincerity only a child could manage. "You, again."

Caroline winced. Oh, dear.

"Me, again." He dropped a deep, flourishing court-worthy bow that earned a giggle as it invariably had when he'd bent one to his own sisters when they'd been younger. To Wynn's credit, he remained perfectly affable and unperturbed by that slight but obvious reminder of his previous connection to their family. To Lettie. "A bad thing or a good?"

Caroline's younger niece made a show of tapping her chin in thoughtful contemplation. "That depends."

He looked hopefully to Caroline. She lifted her lower arms in a lazy shrug.

A wicked glimmer danced in the girl's mischievous eyes. "Do you know any jests?"

"Jests?" he repeated.

"My sister loves jokes," Faith explained.

"Ah." He inclined his head in understanding, then dropping his hands on his knees, so he erased some of the height difference between him and Violet, Wynn asked; "How are young ladies like arrows?"

The younger girl shook her head. "How?"

"Because they are all a'quiver in the presence of a *beau*," he answered, drawing a fit of giggles from the girl, and a laugh from both Faith and Caroline.

He straightened, and then catching Caroline's eyes, he winked, that quick, subtle flutter of his long, inky black lashes that suggested they shared a secret connection. Caroline went absolutely motionless, the smile freezing on her face as this time, she well and truly did lose her heart to Wynn Masterson—this man who engaged so very easily with her young nieces when most people failed to see children at all.

"That is good stuff there, my lord," Violet heaped that not insignificant for her praise upon him. "Most gents don't have any ones they can share with younger ladies."

Faith emitted a nervous laugh. "Violet," she chided her garrulous sibling.

Wynn waved off that worrying and refocused all his attention on Faith. "I've a sister near your age," he explained. "She also has an affinity for a good joke."

Violet's eyes lit up. "Do you have any oth—?"

Interrupting the rest of that request, Faith caught her sister by her spare hand. "Lord Exmoor is otherwise busy."

Violet furrowed her brow. "He's just talking to Aunt—*oww*." She glared at Faith. "Why did you pin—*oww*?"

"It was *so* very wonderful seeing you again," Faith said loudly, over the rest of her sister's grumblings. And then, with an apologetic look for Caroline, she tugged the reluctant girl along.

"Why did you...?" The rest of Violet's dogged question trailed off as they disappeared to the front of the shop, leaving Caroline and Wynn alone once more.

"Thank you," she said. "You were very good with them."

"As I said, I have sisters of my own."

He spoke with an affection Caroline had only ever heard in her own brothers. In a world where so much value was placed upon the male heir and lineage, it was a rarity. "You are close with them," she remarked.

"I would do anything for them." He glanced away; but not before she caught the odd twisting of his features as if he were a man in pain. It was a response gone so quickly she may have imagined it. "I should go," he murmured.

"Don't feel you must." Stay, please.

"Alas, the calling hour," he said, and there was regret there.

The calling hour? Which meant he was calling on... someone else.

"Who?" It emerged a faint, breathless whisper she could not call back, a bold, improper question she'd no right to ask, but one that she'd needed to speak aloud so that she might have an answer. "Who is it you are courting?"

He hesitated, his gaze lingering over the top of Caroline's head. "Lady Beatrice Dennington."

Lady Beatrice Dennington. Not a young debutante. Near in age to Caroline's...but innocent, her reputation unblemished. Perfectly lovely in every way.

The flowers he'd come here to choose...were not for her. They were for another. Mortification swept through her. Of course, they were. *How could I be so foolish? Did I truly think a man such as he would pursue a spinster with a scandal?* And just as awful... she'd spoken to him about her scandal. White hot humiliation and something more, something sharper—pain, gripped her. Why did he have to be so very good with her nieces? It would have been so much easier to dismiss this gravest mistake she'd made had he been curt with children and not so very patient with them.

"Caroline?" His voice came as if down a long tunnel, her name wreathed in concern from a man who'd noted her odd reaction.

She knew she was supposed to assure him she was fine. That everything was fine. Only, it wasn't.

Everything hurt inside. Her heart. Her soul. Her lungs. Was there a single part of her safe from this hurt and humiliation?

What a fool she'd been. To think he might have been thinking about courting her.

"I should see to my nieces," she managed.

There, words.

Caroline wanted to run and hide from the agony of it all. She should curtsy. Propriety dictated it and yet she couldn't bring her muscles to make the movements. Instead, coward that she was, Caroline turned without so much as a goodbye.

And then she stopped.

"Myrtle," she said, her voice hollow to her own ears.

"What?"

She made herself face him once more. "They are the flower of love and marriage. They are the perfect flower for…her." Perfect for another. Perfect for the lady he secured them for.

He hesitated, and unlike before, when he'd lingered and remained, this time he dropped a bow and left with his flowers in hand.

His flowers, for another lady.

His future bride.

CHAPTER 10

SEVERAL DAYS AFTER CAROLINE'S EQUAL parts glorious and equal parts humiliating misunderstanding with Wynn, Caroline sat beside her youngest niece. The girl had her head buried in a book.

As she read, Caroline breathed in the spring air, relishing the escape from her mother's interference and her brother's attempts at making any of it better. Why, even the interest in her fall days earlier had begun to die down. Some.

Yes, she should only feel good this day.

Alas, mortification dogged her still—this time, not because of a fall that hadn't been her fault. But rather, because of the erroneous conclusion she'd drawn at the hothouse.

Had she really believed, even for a single moment that a man such as Wynn would ever court her? Her.

And the worst part of it was…in that instant at the hothouse…she had.

She'd believed he, a man so very patient with young

ladies, devoted to his sisters of whom he spoke affectionately, and with a flawless reputation, would ever find himself so very captivated by Caroline, of all women, that he'd risk the scandal sure to follow were he to court and wed her.

A groan slipped from her lips.

"Are you all right, Aunt Caro?" Violet's concern-laden question reached across Caroline's embarrassment.

"Yes. I...I..." *Have always been deuced bad at prevaricating.* Her gaze lit on a girl in the distance flying a kite. Or attempting to. "I was just noticing the girl is doing it all wrong." Which, as she and now Violet both considered the young, wasn't untrue.

Even as she fumbled with the triangular frame, however, the girl attended the task with all the exuberance and innocence her tender years allowed.

Given the wind whipping about, it should be a fairly easy task.

Or that was likely what one would suspect when flying a kite on a windy spring day.

But it wasn't as easy as all that.

And a wistful longing filled Caroline for when she'd been that person, too, so very carefree that the greatest trouble was the task of getting her kite to take flight.

Violet instantly snapped her book closed. "Do you know how to fly one?"

"I do," she confessed, with surely greater pride than the task merited. And yet, there were so few accomplishments she'd truly had over the years.

Her niece's eyes grew rounded in a blend of surprise and admiration. "Indeed?" she pressed, scooting closer.

"Oh, yes. There is a certain skill to it." One Caroline had possessed in spades. Where her sisters had been hopeless to make those cloth scraps fly, she'd unfailingly gotten hers to take flight and remain there, a stark white flag soaring against the crisp blue Somerset sky.

It was an odd detail to note, as it had been years since she'd done it herself.

And one surely forgot.

And yet...Ironically, Caroline had *not* forgotten.

"You must show her."

It took a moment to register Violet had spoken, and what she was saying.

The girl gestured to the kite-flier. "Lord knows her governess isn't doing her any good."

The young girl's governess sat at her ward's side with a book in hand and her head down over it while the child attempted in vain to get that article into the sky.

She wrestled with the silk kite that climbed several inches above the ground before falling, nose first, for the earthen floor.

Even with the twenty or so paces between them, Caroline caught the noisy, less than polite, mutterings of the frustrated flier. The wind carried both those shockingly naughty curses and the occasional rote scolding the charge's governess murmured, all as she read and the girl sought to get her kite aloft.

From over the top of the needlepoint she'd brought, Caroline smiled wistfully on at that girl, shades of her long-forgotten self, peeking out from the overly cautious woman she'd become. She recalled herself uttering those same curses, alongside her equally naughty sister, Lettie.

Her smile slipped, and she pulled her gaze away from that fun activity she'd once enjoyed to the less enjoyable one that she'd been expected to pick up, as all ladies did. She'd initially resisted because she'd so preferred being outdoors and running about.

...who will marry a girl with grass stains upon her skirt, and bloodstains on her fingers, from your absolute ineptitude with a needle, Caroline Rose...

Those long-ago lamentations slipped in as fresh as if it had been yesterday and not two thousand yesterdays.

Eventually, Caroline had triumphed. Because she'd so dedicated herself to triumphing in even those miserable tasks assigned by her mother. For Caroline had known, all of that misery with the dowager marchioness was temporary, and there'd be a loving husband who'd whisk Caroline away from that oppressive weight always bearing down on her.

How ironic to now find herself all these years later a spinster so on the shelf that she'd watched not only her two sisters but two brothers marry and had herself remained unwed.

"It's bloody impossible." Another gust of spring wind carried that frustrated cry over, crisp and clear, breaking across Caroline's melancholy musings.

"...perhaps it is time we leave, and try another..." The governess's occasional urgings peppered the air. "...return for your lessons and then..."

"*No*. I must not quit. I almost have it."

"The girl does not almost have it," Violet noted, matter-of-factly.

"No," Caroline murmured. She wasn't even close.

"Just a moment more." The girl's entreaty rang out as clear as the bells of Westminster Abbey. "I *hate* needlepoint," she wailed, and Caroline's gaze slipped down once more to the frame held between her hands.

...but I hate needlepoint, Mama...It is boring...

Her own long-ago lamentations melded and merged

with the young girl's and Caroline found her gaze slipping up and out once more. Transfixed, she stared unblinkingly at the child, and in those moments, she saw the girl years later, a bitter, less fun, miserable version of the person she was now.

The person who now laughed freely, without attempting to stifle those exuberant sounds. Who jested and ran wild across parks and grounds, tempered then so that her steps were careful and measured and practiced to the point of pain.

Her chest tightened, and she was suffocating.

Nay, she'd already suffocated, but it was happening all over again.

Only, this time she realized it, saw the world closing in, and tightening about her and—

The girl dropped the kite to her side. "Oh, very well," she said with a tangible resignation. "I will do my needlepoint, but you must promise we will return."

There would be no returning.

The kite would go in a drawer in the nursery, and then the needlepoint would come out, and it would never go away. It would begin a new flag, only a small one that did not fly high or twist and whip in the wind, but rather one that stayed between her fingers, while her feet remained planted firmly on the ground and—

Before she could stop herself, Caroline called out. "You're doing it wrong!" She'd raised her voice loud enough to earn the stares of passing strangers. This time, unlike all the other moments before in her life, she didn't pay them any heed.

Violet let out a little whoop. "Huzzah! You're going to do it!"

The other little girl turned her attention squarely on

Caroline. "Beg pardon?"

Dropping her needlepoint, Caroline climbed to her feet and collecting her hems she started forward. Violet followed closely at her side. "Your kite," Caroline explained.

"You know how to fly a kite?"

Violet piped in before Caroline could. "Oh, my aunt is most good at it." Her niece's avowal, based on nothing more than the words Caroline had given her, rang with pride.

Caroline had grown so accustomed to the world's contempt, both girls' admiration at her 'abilities' proved a welcome change, one that left her feeling light.

"Indeed?" the child asked, looking with renewed interest at Caroline.

"I've had some experience," she confessed.

Eager excitement lit the child's pretty brown eyes. "Will you show me?"

She and Violet spoke as one.

"Absolutely, she will."

Caroline reflexively brought her palms up. "I couldn't." As in, she really could not. Young ladies did not go running about Hyde Park. Ladies did not run at all. Spinsters with ruined reputations, especially not. "I can, however, explain—"

"Why can't you?"

The girl's bluntly honest question brought Caroline up short.

"Yes…why?" Violet pleaded with her eyes.

Caroline opened her mouth to speak on the rules of propriety but stopped before those words could fully form and materialize on her tongue. She puzzled her brow. The girls were right? Why couldn't she?

Since her scandal, she'd conducted herself above

reproach, and what had that gotten her?

Caroline smiled. "Do you know, I cannot think of a single good reason."

Both girls of a like height, but different coloring, cocked their heads in a comically similar way.

Caroline clarified. "That is, I cannot think of a single good reason as to why I shouldn't."

The girl clapped her hands happily. "Huzzah! Now, you must tell me."

"Well, you see…" She paused, looking for the girls' name.

"Elspeth," her apprentice offered, sinking into a perfect curtsy.

"I'm Violet," her niece hurried to introduce herself to her new fast friend.

"Well, you see, Elspeth," Caroline resumed her lesson, "the secret is pointing the bridle up." Caroline held her arms at the correct angle, demonstrating the positioning for her eager student. "And you must let the line out, so."

As she spoke, Elspeth and Violet stared on wide-eyed, nodding, and repeating back the instructions, clarifying her understanding.

Caroline's mother had long bemoaned the fact that her daughter-in-law, Miles's wife, the Marchioness of Guilford, had opened a school for young girls who with their hearing and visual difficulties were invariably shunned by society. Caroline hadn't given much thought to that venture, one way or the other. Until now. Until doling out a kite lesson, Caroline at last appreciated fully what her sister-in-law, Philippa, in fact did, and how very wonderful it felt.

Granted, you're just teaching a kite-flying lesson, a droll voice in her head reminded her.

And yet, she was passing on joy, and in this instant, as a woman who knew anything but that sentiment herself anymore, she couldn't imagine anything more important.

"But is there sufficient wind?" Violet asked.

"Certainly, more than enough," their new-found friend assured. "My older brother flies it with far less."

The girl had a brother. One who took time to fly kites, just as Rhys and Miles had done with her and their sisters.

"No. You are correct," Caroline confirmed the girl's assertion. Lifting a palm over her eyes to shield them from the sun, so she could better see the girl, she shared all her remembering about kite-flying. "The trick is to let the kite fly away from you a little. Yes, just like that," she praised as her new student followed those instructions. "A bit more. Now release more of the line." Elspeth released a tad too much, and the kite dipped. "It is a slow process. As you let it climb and it begins to ascend, you must pull on the line as the kite points up."

Both girls listened intently to those directions, their cherubically rounded faces scrunched up in a like, deep concentration, and Caroline stared wistfully at the pair, quietly, casually conversing as they flew the kite.

They were what Caroline would have wished for her daughter to be, and the games she would have played with her. If there'd been a daughter. If there'd been *any* child.

But there were nieces and nephews, and Lettie would have babes, and she'd take care of them. And that would be enough.

She was a horrid liar. Even to herself.

"You never said what your name is," Elspeth said, glancing over.

Emotion filled her throat.

"I am Caroline." When was the last time she'd given another person her Christian name? When was the last time anyone wished for it? Only...

"...given our family's connection, I expect it would be fine to use one another's Christian names..."

Her gut clenched as memories of that night at the Duke and Duchess of Crawford's slipped in. The evening Wynn had been running his hands over her legs.

"Aunt Caro?" her niece's concerned tone slashed across those pitiable musings.

"Forgive me," she blurted. "Where were we?"

The girl's smile was firmly back in place. "You were going to show Elspeth how to fly the kite."

A slow smile brought Caroline's lips up. Yes, she was.

"If I may?" she said, and collecting the kite once more, she pointed the bride up, and let her line out as she'd previously instructed. And it was as though no time had passed at all. She let the kite fly away from her a little, then pointed it upward at the sky. It began its climb.

"You're doing it!" Elspeth cried.

Violet's echoing laugh peeled around the park. "She certainly is!"

Concentrating on the task at hand, Caroline bit at her lower lip, reading the wind and the kite's placement, and slowly releasing more slack, feeding it out, until it soared high above the ground—a flag whipping in the spring breeze.

A triumphant laugh slipped out, both exultant and stunned.

She had forgotten what it felt to do anything for the simple joy of doing.

"You must run, Aunt Caro," Violet shouted. "It is the only way. *Run.*"

Both little girls cried out together, "Run!"

Run.

And then...Caroline did.

Slowly at first, her every step measured, a million and one lectures doled out from her mother and governesses of old playing in her mind, and then fading as Elspeth's laughter drowned out those whiny echoes. Running in Hyde Park. It was scandalous. It was improper. It was... *freeing*.

And it felt so very good. With every step, she found herself dashing further and further away from the demands placed upon her and dashing with increasing speed towards a place where she'd once loved to dwell, and a place she'd not been in so long—a place of jubilance and joy, where she didn't care who watched her, if anyone did.

And she didn't care about her mother's lectures on ladylike propriety.

Her heart thundering and pounding, Caroline increased the speed of her steps. And then she broke free of those constraints all together. Allowing the kite's movements to dictate the speed with which she moved, she increased the cadence of her feet, darting to the left and the right when the wind warranted a shift in direction.

Until the kite, at last, gained the altitude and her breath caught, and she stared on at the wisp of fabric so much smaller against the crisp blue sky, waving like a white flag.

Caroline watched the kite wave back and forth.

I did it...

"You've done it." Those whispered words of the girl beside her, and she glanced down at Elspeth.

That distraction cost her.

Violet waved frantically at the sky. "It is falling," she cried.

Caroline whipped her gaze skyward.

Sure enough, the kite now faltered, slipping left and right.

Furrowing her brow, Caroline concentrated on tugging the string, and then she set off running.

The little girls' combined cheer echoed around the grounds once more, and it invigorated Caroline; filling her with a lightness, and drawing laughter from her, as she raced backwards, in a bid to keep the kite aloft.

And it was.

Laughter spilling from her lips, Caroline glanced back over her shoulder as she went.

"Huzzah, you are doing it again, Caroline." Her child-champion lifted her arms high above her head, and joining her hands, she shook them. Suddenly, Violet and Elspeth's eyes widened and panic lit their faces. They again spoke as one, "You are going to—"

Crash.

Caroline collided headfirst with a solid, unyielding brick wall.

She gasped as the air left her lungs. The force of the collision loosened her hold on the kite, and she went flying forward.

With a groan, Caroline lay dazed.

This was why a lady did not run.

This—

She opened her eyes…and froze.

Nay, she'd been wrong.

This was why *she* did not run.

This, right here.

She'd run head-first, not into a stone wall, but rather

the wall of muscle that was the gentleman's chest.

Him.

Not just *any* gentleman.

"You," she blurted.

He offered a wan smile. "Me," he said, as though it were the most natural thing in the world to find himself flat on his back in the middle of Hyde Park, with her draped over him.

His hooded gaze slid over her face, dipping lower, to the bodice of her serviceable dress, lingering there, before finding her eyes with his once more.

And his wasn't the repulsed gaze.

Nay, in fact, he looked at her as no man had ever looked at her. Ever. Not even the Earl of Somerville.

Wynn's mesmerizing blue-eyed stare was filled with desire.

Her heart raced. Faster.

And her chest rose and fell in time to his equally labored breathing.

This time, a different heat stole over her body, not one of humiliation and shame, but longing.

Of their own volition, her hands came up, and she pressed them against the firm wall of his chest, curling them in the fabric of his sapphire blue jacket.

The smell of him.

It was raw and real and masculine, an earthy, wood smell of bergamot and citrusy blend of orange that in their shared time at the hothouse she'd failed to note because of the overwhelming scent of the flowers they'd then explored together.

Now, with the earth standing still, she breathed deep of him; closing her eyes, and inhaling the heady scent, wanting to lose herself in him and in this moment.

She let her lashes flutter open so she could drink in the sight of his face, once more.

And then promptly wished she hadn't.

Horror. Now that was an all too familiar, far more recognizable sentiment.

The world resumed its spinning, in a rapid way.

With a gasp, she rolled herself off of him, toppling sideways and onto the grass.

"Are you hurt?" Wynn asked.

Unable to tamp down a groan, Caroline closed her eyes, and let her head fall back onto the thick lawn.

Bloody damnation on Sunday.

THE FIRST TIME WYNN NOTICED Caroline Brookfield had been weeks earlier inside a hothouse shop when he'd been selecting flowers for the lady's sister whom he'd been courting at the time.

He'd only noted Caroline because he'd happened to glance over and saw the sun playing through the glass-ceiling, and she'd had her face tipped up towards the ray slanting through those lead panes. She'd put him in mind of a kitten stretching toward the sun. And he'd been enthralled. He'd also felt like the worst sort of cad for having so noticed the sister of a lady whom he'd been courting.

He'd forced himself to not think of her as she'd been or that day, ever again, and when he'd been courting Lady Lettie it had been easier. For every time he'd seen Caroline thereafter, she'd been as she'd always been before that moment—somber. Serious. And he'd missed her as she'd been when her face ran red with color at her happiness.

But then, just recently, there'd been that time in the garden centre when Caroline had given him a riveting lesson on the meaning of various flowers.

Her cheeks had bloomed with color from her laugh.

Just as they were now.

Only, there was no longer a courtship.

At least, not to her sister. There was a handful of visits he'd paid to Lady Beatrice…

And now this new, fresher, and very dangerous remembrance of Caroline Brookfield, her laughter filling the park as she had played freely with his sister and her niece.

An angry cry ripped across the grounds and wrenched him from his dazed state.

With a quiet curse, Wynn jumped up.

"I will never, ever forgive you, Wynn." His sister's shout ripped across his shocked musings, and he looked over as Elspeth raced towards the woman still sprawled on the ground. "You have killed Caroline."

"I am not dead," Lady Caroline assured, and then muttered something under her breath that sounded a good deal like, *'I only wish I was'*.

A smile twitched at his lips.

Caroline closed her eyes and groaned. "Oh, no."

Elspeth giggled. "My brother has that effect on women. Isn't that right, Wynn?"

His grin slipped, and he looked back to Caroline. He stretched out a hand.

The lady gasped. She scooted out of his reach, scrambling backwards on her buttocks in a way certain to leave grass stains upon her skirts. "What are you doing?" she squawked.

"I think he's trying to help you, Aunt Caro," Violet

whispered noisily.

Wynn nodded. "I'm helping you stand?" Or he'd been trying to.

"That will not be necessary," she said on a rush, and made to rise.

Wynn frowned. "I insist."

Only, she moved far out of his reach, eyeing his hands with something akin to horror.

"She doesn't want your help, Wynn," Elspeth snapped; her devotion having swiftly transferred that day to Lady Caroline. "Because you almost killed her."

"*Accidentally* almost killed her," Violet put in that clarifying point.

"He did not almost kill me," Caroline said weakly, and her gaze slipped away, beyond Wynn, his sister, her niece, and over to Denbigh who was looking on with far too much interest and enjoyment for Wynn's liking.

And then Wynn followed her stare. Not to Denbigh.

Rather to the sizeable crowd they'd drawn.

And his stomach knotted as did every other muscle in his person as the lady's mutterings about a preferred death at last made sense.

Every nearby voyeur gawked on, making no attempt to feign their rabid fascination.

And he knew precisely what they saw, and even worse, he knew precisely what they would say about this particular woman having run square into him.

He dimly registered Denbigh rushing forward to help Caroline up, and a peculiar annoyance tightened in his gut at the sight of his friend's fingers tangled with hers.

Whatever the earl said just then pulled a laugh from Caroline, and Wynn's unpleasant feeling grew, spreading like a poison, souring his tongue.

"Lady Caroline, I cannot thank you enough for helping my sister," Wynn said loudly, awkwardly interrupting that intimate exchange.

As if she'd forgotten his presence, and only just recalled him standing there, Caroline looked over.

"You needn't thank me." She met his gaze with a directness that intrigued. His heart thumped weirdly. Her interest in him lasted no longer than a moment. She switched her attention to Elspeth. "I had a lovely time with Elspeth and Violet," she said softly, and then dipped a curtsy. "But I really should be returning."

"Must you go?" Elspeth implored, and he found himself oddly wishing for Caroline to remain; wanting his sister's pleas to work.

"Please, Aunt Caro," Violet begged.

Caroline's features softened. "I'm afraid I must," she murmured. She offered her thanks to Denbigh.

He inclined his head. "It was my pleasure, my lady."

Wynn gritted his teeth. His pleasure. He'd bet it was.

Caroline slid her attention once more over to Wynn's, reluctant in a way she'd not been with Denbigh.

That grated, too.

"My lord," she said softly, and then collecting her hems, she made to go.

He stared after her. It was best she went.

He was to wed another. Why, he'd already called on Lady Beatrice, and though not overly passionate about his visits, Wynn had started himself on the path of courtship and then marriage, and—

"Must you?" he called out, and it was harder to say who was more stunned by that question.

He. Denbigh. Or Lady Caroline, who whipped back around.

His sister and her niece, on the other hand, let out jubilant cries, and Violet bounded back over.

Caroline hesitated before venturing over once more.

When she reached him, Wynn cleared his throat. "That is, thank you. I'm really quite rubbish at flying—"

"No, you're *ffnoff*." The four fingers he slid over his sister's mouth muffled the rest of that admission.

From the corner of his eye, Wynn caught Denbigh lounging against the enormous trunk of a willow tree, his arms folded at his chest, and looking entirely too amused by the exchange.

Undeterred, Elspeth pushed his hand away. "He's not rubbish at flying kites." She lifted a finger up to the cloudless London sky. "He is, however, rubbish at *teaching* someone how to fly them."

Wynn caught Caroline's gaze. "Gathering the praise my sisters heap upon me, it's a wonder my head isn't swelled."

Her lips twitched upwards in one of those smiles that absolutely transformed her, riveting him, holding him spellbound.

Elspeth gave his hand a devoted sisterly pat. "You are good at a very many things. Isn't that right, Denbigh?" she called over to the earl.

"Indeed," his friend said, tipping the brim of his hat.

Having secured that support, Elspeth put her appeal to Wynn. "You must show Lady Caroline how you can fly a kite."

His sister and Lady Violet jumped up and down, clapping their hands, urging him on. Wynn looked over the tops of their heads at Caroline. Her eyes sparkled when he'd never known eyes really could glimmer with that bright light.

He should decline. There were a thousand and one

reasons he should decline. And only one to stay—he wanted to be here with Caroline.

Despite logic and reason and expectations and everything which told him to go, he instead found himself reaching for the kite.

Cheers erupted from Elspeth and Lady Violet; but it was Caroline who gave an equally eager little clap who held him enthralled. It took a Herculean effort to pull his eyes from her and force his gaze instead to the bridle of the kite.

Wynn held it out, waiting for it to catch the wind and then as it did, he gradually released the line.

"Huzzah!" Lady Violet hailed.

As it climbed higher and higher, he made sure the line wasn't slack, keeping it slightly taut.

"I told you he could fly a kite," Elspeth said to the other girl and Caroline, all while Wynn moved farther and farther back to ensure he kept the child's toy aloft. "I merely pointed out that he isn't so very good at teaching a person how to do it. Hence his not explaining just exactly what he did to get the kite up there."

Wynn pulled his focus from the sky and looked over at the trio of ladies who made up his audience. "The trick is in—"

Looks of matching horror rounded out three sets of eyes.

Denbigh and Caroline called out warnings at the same time. "Exmoor!"

"Tree!"

Wynn yanked his gaze back to the kite, just as it collided with a branch.

His friend slapped a hand over his eyes.

Silence replaced his previously jubilant admirers' happy

laughter.

"Er, mayhap he can't fly a kite?" Lady Violet whispered loudly.

Caroline's lips twitched, as she rested a hand on her niece's shoulder.

Elspeth found her voice. "My kite," she cried, racing over. Caroline and Violet came to join her at the foot of the tree.

Shielding his eyes, Wynn looked up. "It's—"

"Tangled?" Caroline supplied for him.

"I was going to say not tangled badly," he drawled.

They shared a smile.

"All depends on one's idea of badly," Denbigh called over from that tree he still lounged against, looking entirely too amused.

Wynn shot him an annoyed look, which only earned another round of laughter.

His sister set her jaw mutinously and reached for a slightly too-high-for-her branch.

"Whoa." Wynn caught her gently by the hand. "What do you think you are doing?"

"What does it look like I'm doing?" she asked on a huff. "I'm going to fetch it."

"You are not climbing a tree."

"I *always* climb trees," she shot back.

He lowered his voice. "At our homes and in the country." When she was wearing trousers and boots, not slippers and skirts. He took care to not mention as much. "Not here in the middle of Hyde Park," he settled for instead.

His sister wrinkled her nose. "It's not really the middle as much as the back portion of it, and I'm a good deal better at climbing trees than you are at flying kites."

Caroline laughed. The sound of her mirth full and rich, not the tittering of measured laughter affected by so many ladies, suddenly had him tongue-tied when he'd never been tongue-tied before.

Elspeth took advantage of his distraction and made another grab for the branch.

Oh, bloody hell. "I'll do it," he muttered, and hefted himself up on the hefty lower limb.

"Are you sure that's a good idea, chap?" Denbigh called over.

"You're welcome to fetch it if you'd like."

His friend grinned. "I'll politely decline, as I'm enjoying the show immensely."

With a sigh, Wynn hefted himself up, and began his ascent.

As he did, Lady Violet's skeptical-rich query reached him. "Are you certain he can climb trees?"

"After his poor showing with the kite, I'm not sure of anything anymore," his sister confessed.

"I heard that," he called, glancing down to where Caroline and the two girls waited.

She said something to them, and they scurried back several steps. "And I saw that," he added dryly.

Violet cupped her hands around her mouth and called out loudly, "That was my Aunt Caro's idea. She pointed out if you fell that we really didn't want to be caught under you."

Wynn paused, and with a hand firmly on a sturdy branch, he sketched a slight bow. "Thank you for your confidence in my abilities, my lady."

Caroline inclined her head. "As your sister pointed out...the whole kite-flying thing." She followed that with a wink.

That light feeling suffused his chest, and he grinned; a smile that felt dizzy and dazed.

"Well, get on with it," his sister prodded, forcing him back to the task at hand. "Unless you want me to, after all?"

Wynn set to work untangling the triangular fabric from the branch it had become tangled with. A moment later he'd managed to free it. His efforts were met with more of the jubilant cheers from before, and as he made the slow descent, his eyes remained locked on a beaming Caroline; her cheeks full of color; her eyes sparkling as they did, and as she joined her fists and hefted them above her head like he was some great conqueror, something shifted within him.

The very earth, it moved under him.

No, wait.

That wasn't the earth.

He stilled.

Caroline flared those enormously round blue eyes.

Wynn cursed and made a futile attempt to catch the nearest limb. His efforts proved in vain.

He found himself tumbling several feet.

Caroline pushed the two younger girls farther from harm, just as Wynn knocked into her.

They toppled to the ground; her cheeks whitened, and an unuttered gasp formed on her lips. In one swift motion, Wynn reversed their positioning, taking the brunt of the impact.

Caroline landed sprawled over him, their chests touching, her limbs pressed against his, and every single thought was knocked from his head, not because of the fall, but because of the feel of her. Her breathing grew more rapid; he heard it in the slight intake of her breath as much as he felt it. Her lashes fluttered; her rosebud-shaped lips trembled.

Wynn lifted his head to take her generous mouth.

"Aunt Caroline!"

All the color left Caroline's cheeks as she scrambled to get up, planting her hands on his chest to propel herself upright.

Denbigh rushed over. "Let me help you, my lady."

As Caroline found her feet with Denbigh's help, a preternatural quiet filled the park, and then like a swarm of bees had been unleashed, a buzzing arose, eating up that previous silence.

With a mix of dread and horror, Wynn looked to the latest crowd he and Caroline had managed to gather around them. A dozen or so ladies and gentlemen who looked on with a vicious glee the way they might have assessed a carriage wreck. Which in fairness, him falling on top of Caroline wasn't much different from those horrific accidents.

"Forgive me," he said quietly.

Caroline gave her head a slight shake. "It's fine." Her lips formed those words perfectly, and yet they remained soundless, too.

"Aunt Caro." Lady Violet brushed past Wynn and Denbigh and grabbed her aunt's hand. "Are you all right?"

And despite the gossips swarming around them and the humiliation of the moment, in what was the most selfless act to assure the child, Caroline mustered a smile. "I'm perfectly fine."

She wasn't, and yet somehow, for her niece, she'd made it sound as though she was. He was completely, hopelessly, and helplessly taken with her.

Something moved within him. Something more

dangerous than the fall he'd suffered, and he found himself taking a fall of a different, far more dangerous sort.

"Must you go?" Elspeth begged Caroline and Lady Violet.

"I'm afraid we must," Caroline said gently. "But perhaps you and Violet might play again one day." She looked to Denbigh, who dropped a swift bow.

"My lady."

She offered a curtsy and a murmur of thanks for his earlier assistance, and then she left.

Wynn followed her proud, noble retreat as she marched through that throng of observers who parted for her, the regal queen she was.

And he found himself lingering his stare upon her gently curved hips, swaying as she walked, and a wave of hungering hit him as—

"What in blazes is wrong with you?" someone demanded.

His sister, he thought. Everything was a bit muddled at the moment. And he felt his cheeks and neck go hot for having been caught.

"I…" Wynn gave his head a clearing shake.

"You *fell* on her," his sister whispered furiously.

And that brought him crashing right back to earth. Wynn winced.

"He most certainly did," Denbigh drawled.

His youngest sister frowned. "And now she's gone, and I was rather enjoying their company and you went and not only ruined it; you knocked Caroline square on her arse."

Denbigh cleared his throat. "If I may be so good as to point out—"

"You may."

"You may not," Wynn said at the same time as his sister's answer for the earl who went on anyway.

"Exmoor knocked Lady Caroline down." The earl shot up two fingers. "Twice today?"

Wynn paused only long enough to glare at the other man before retraining his attention on his youngest sister. Out the corner of his eye, he caught the way the governess dropped her head into her hands. "You should not say that."

Elspeth puzzled her brow. "What? You did knock her down."

"No. No. the other part. Your choice of wor—"

"Arse?"

He winced, and his sister's governess squeezed her eyes shut and gave her head a shake.

Of course, it was hardly the governess's fault. His sister's spirits could not be tamed. Though in fairness, not that he was looking to have her tamed, just not swear like a sailor on Sunday.

"You are lecturing me on my word choice." Planting her hands upon her hips, Elspeth took a furious step towards him, then another, and another, until Wynn was forced to retreat. "You, who go about knocking down young ladies, costing me my best kite instructor ever?"

"He does have something of a habit of continuing to meet in such a way with the lady," Denbigh drawled, and Wynn silently cursed. His sister hadn't yet pieced together the identity of the woman she'd been keeping company with, and he preferred to keep it that way.

Elspeth switched her attention to the earl. "What are you jabbering about."

"Do not," Wynn said tightly, his efforts to silence the other man and end his discourse with Elspeth in vain.

Worse than London's busiest gossip, Denbigh slid closer, and whispered, "The lady in question was none other than Lady Caroline."

Dead. He was going to kill his friend dead.

Elspeth froze, and then widened her eyes. Then recognition registered. "*The* Lady Caroline. The same Lady Caroline whom you refused to catch at the Duke and Duchess of Crawford's ball?"

"None other," Denbigh said.

"I didn't refuse to catch her," Wynn muttered. He'd failed to do so. Which was an equally egregious affront.

Then the impossible happened. His sister went silent. There *were* small miracles to be had that day.

It lasted but an instant.

His sister marched the remainder of the way, jabbing at the air with her finger as she went. "Wynn Masterson, you are rude and unforgiveable and boorish."

He winced. Yes, he was deserving of all that.

"It's one thing to fail to catch her,"—*That had been bad enough*—"which is bad enough." Yes, he quite agreed with her there. "But falling on her?"

His muscles seized once more. He'd only brought more gossip to Caroline, further humiliation that she didn't deserve. Which belonged not to her mother this time, but squarely with Wynn.

Yes, indeed, that was precisely what he'd done. Inadvertently. But humiliate her all the same. This time, for a third time, in front of a sea of respectable members of Polite Society, who were no doubt already running about with the tale of his latest run-in with Lady Caroline.

And yet, as he and his sister gathered up her things and together with Denbigh prepared to make their own escape from Hyde Park, Wynn discovered he was more selfish than he'd ever believed himself to be, for he could not regret the time he'd spent here with Caroline this morning.

CHAPTER 11

SOCIETY MIGHT FORGIVE A WOMAN who'd humiliated herself with an accidental fall.

They *might*.

What they would never tolerate was a woman who flung herself at a man. They'd tolerate it even less when said woman flung herself at a man who'd begun courting one of society's beloveds. And there could be no doubting, Lady Beatrice, with her beauty, connections, and notorious warmness was, in fact, a beloved.

Or that was what was being said, following Caroline's exchanges with Wynn at Hyde Park. Desperate to wed, and one who'd proven herself scandalous in the past, she'd think nothing of creating another scandal if it meant she could this time snag herself a husband.

Caroline studied the inside of her fan.

She was never going out again.

Ever.

The gossip about her latest fall in front of Wynn had raced with such fire through London's parlors that not even Caroline's mother had sought to drag her out to save face. Rather, the dowager marchioness had gone off on her own this night to put on a brave show and enlist the support of her fellow miserable matrons, as Caroline had come to think of the dowager's friends through the years.

As such, with her mother gone and Caroline granted a reprieve from those miserable social events, one could actually say that some good had come from her latest scandal, after all—a gathering between the Brookfields and Edgertons, Philippa's steadfast and loyal family.

"It *must* be Caro," her sister Lettie, seated beside her new husband, Anthony, the Duke of Granville, called across the parlor.

The adults stomped their feet, lending their noisy support to Lettie's suggestion.

"Aunt Caro isn't even paying attention," Violet lamented.

"I am so," she said defensively. "I'm merely examining my options." She turned her fan around quickly so the assembled Brookfields and their respective spouses and children could assess the charade riddles written inside her folding fan.

"I will go until she's ready," Paddy cried, clapping his hands.

"You just went, scamp." Violet tugged one of his blonde curls. "Why don't you allow Cousin Rowan to go?"

From where he sat on the window seat reading, Rowan, the Marquess and Marchioness of Tennyson's eldest son, didn't even look out from behind his book. "I'm entirely too old to play children's games."

Rowan's sister, Rose, pulled a face. "I'm entirely to *ooooold* to play children's games," she mimicked in a near perfect impersonation of the boy. "You're *eight*, Rowan."

Jumping up and down to make himself heard over that bickering, Paddy waved his arms wildly. "Pleaaase let me!"

Caroline stared on wistfully at the bucolic display of her happy family. It was the most normal life had been in so very long that one could almost forget Caroline was being talked about once more.

Liar. You don't give a fig about that. Rather, it's the fact you enjoyed every moment spent with Wynn Masterson, the Marquess of Exmoor, even as he'd begun courting another woman. That dratted know-it-all voice again.

Philippa gave her hands a clap, reigning in her younger children, as all assembled Brookfields and Edgertons gave her their full attention. "The only thing to be done in a situation such as this..." Paddy and Violet leaned to the edges of their seats, hanging on their mother's announcement. Philippa shifted her focus to Miles. "Is for your father to have his turn."

Cheers went up around the room, and their fight over the next round of charades was forgotten as Paddy and Violet joined their aunt and uncle, Chloe and Leo, the Marquess and Marchioness of Tennyson, in their amusement.

Miles slumped in his seat. "You are all gluttons for humiliating me," he groaned.

"Indeed we are, dear brother." Rhys gave his brother a hearty thump between the shoulder blades.

Together, Lord Tennyson and Rhys joined in catching Miles by the arms and propelling him to his feet.

And for the first time since the backlash she'd received for those exchanges in Hyde Park with Wynn, Caroline found herself smiling.

"A penny for your thoughts."

Caroline started and looked up at her younger sister Lettie who'd made her way over.

Lettie smiled. "Make some space, now, will you?" Her sister softened that command with a wink.

Caroline scooted over.

They sat together watching and laughing as Miles bumbled through another poor attempt at charades, and it felt so very good to laugh and play games and for even just a short time forget how awful everything truly was.

"Here, let me see that," Lettie said, plucking Caroline's fan from her fingers. Propping it open, she held the satin article to their eye level so they could evaluate the charade clues penned upon the fabric. "You had the right of it before," she whispered. "One can snag a moment of privacy this way."

They shared a soft laugh, so very reminiscent of the giggles of their youth when life had been so much easier.

Lettie's smile slipped, and she moved her gaze over Caroline's face. "I...wanted to speak with you about Lord Exmoor."

Around a particularly noisy swell from the family over Miles's antics, it took a moment before her sister's quietly spoken statement registered.

Caroline dampened her mouth. "Lord Exmoor?" she repeated, carefully.

Lettie leaned closer. "I don't take care what the gossip pages say about anything," she said earnestly. "But there was mention of you and him in Hyde Park."

"With Violet and his sister, Elspeth," Caroline quietly interrupted. "It was an innocent meeting." To him. To her, it had been one of the most joyous moments she'd known—since her previous interactions with him. "The newspapers are merely making more of it than there is."

"Yes, I trust that," Lettie rushed to assure her. "It is just...what I am trying to say...what I wanted to say..." She caught Caroline's hand. "If you do have feelings for the marquess, feelings that go back to," a blush stained her younger sister's cheeks, "when he was courting me."—Odd, it should cut like a knife to be reminded of Wynn's interest in her sister—"I would have never encouraged him or his suit as I'd never do anything to hurt you. Ever."

No, Caroline believed that implicitly. "Lettie," Caroline said with the same firmness she'd used when they'd been girls in the nursery, and she'd sought to set the rules of their play. "In case you forget, I encouraged you to consider Lord Exmoor." Because she'd known he was a man who was honorable and good, and that he'd treat Lettie well. She knew he'd be for Lettie all Caroline had ever wanted in a husband.

Her sister offered a sad smile. "Yes, that is true. But you're also a selfless sister. If you believed the marquess would make me a good husband, I don't doubt you'd sacrifice your own happiness."

"You give me more credit than I deserve." Unable to meet Lettie's eyes, Caroline lowered the fan they'd used as cover and made a show of watching her brother crawling about the floor as whatever animal he pretended to be for the latest round of charades. "If I was truly selfless, I would not have thrown away my reputation,"—*and virtue*—"on a bounder, and risked your future, as I did."

Lettie took her fingers. "Look at me." She applied a slight, but firm pressure to Caroline's hand, forcing Caroline to meet her gaze. "You are not to blame for what Lord Somerville did. I do not blame you."—She night not. But Caroline blamed herself and with good reason—"I never did, Caroline, and I never will." Her sister leaned close and whispered. "If anything, I should thank you for securing me a reprieve in having my debut all those years ago." She gave a playful waggle of her eyebrows, and Caroline found herself laughing.

Her younger sister put an arm around her shoulder and drew her in for a hug. "That is better."

They rested their heads against one another's and watched their family at play. Another swell of laughter went up around the parlor over Miles's latest charade antics.

"What do you think," Lettie drawled. "Is there anyone worse at charades than Miles?"

Caroline snorted. "Not a one in the whole kingdom."

Miles looked up. "I heard that," he called over.

"You aren't allowed to speak, Papa," Violet chided, prodding her father back to the game.

And as Lettie and everyone switched all their attention back to Miles, Caroline found herself grateful for the cessation of questions about her past scandal that made any possibility of a future with Wynn impossible.

CHAPTER 12

She was so close.

So close to freedom.

Given the early morn hour, it should not be a difficult task. At this time, when the sun hadn't even made an appearance, Caroline should have been permitted to sneak off, and escape.

Alas, she wasn't even to be granted a trip to Hyde Park without a lecture.

"Do you see what they are saying about you now?"

That crisp demand from behind her shoulder froze Caroline in her tracks, and she stared longingly at the door, eying the handle a moment.

So close.

And yet, also so very far away.

Her family's butler gave her a commiserative look, as Caroline turned to greet her mother.

"Good morning, Mother," she murmured.

"Good morning. *Good morning?*" her mother echoed her own crisp words. "It most certainly is not a good morning." She brandished the latest set of gossip pages. "In fact, it is anything but."

Caroline's stomach fell.

"Have you seen this?" her mother demanded waving them in front of Caroline's face.

"I haven't," she said. That had been, after all, the plan. To try and escape before the papers arrived.

She was going to have to start getting out of this household even earlier now.

"They are saying you are shameless in your desperation," her mother seethed.

White hot humiliation speared her. There was no escaping her past. It mattered not that she'd conducted herself in a way that even her mother couldn't have found fault with these past years. All the world would ever see was the one thing Caroline had done wrong.

"How could you do this?" Her mother shoved those papers at Caroline.

"I've done nothing," she gritted out, refusing to collect them. The only thing she had done was make herself a dutiful daughter and respectable lady, and what had that gotten her, beyond scorn?

"That is it precisely," her mother pounced. "It was bad enough that you ruined your good name with that fortune hunter all those years ago. But now, you'd humiliate yourself and this family by throwing yourself at a gentleman who is courting *the* Lady Beatrice."

Shame twisted through Caroline and the self-control she'd spent a lifetime sharpening snapped.

At her side, she caught the glances her maid and the family butler slid her way, and found herself grounded in that show of support; and she found her voice. "You are the one who has done this," she hissed. Her mother's eyebrows went shooting up. "Not me. You." Her mother, who thought nothing of speaking of this latest embarrassment she'd suffered in the presence of servants. "Need I remind you that you pushed me at him, Mother. *You*."

"Perhaps if you'd fallen with any dignity or grace we'd not be in this very situation," her mother wailed. "How was I to have known that all those years of practice had not done you any good." Her mother hurled the pages at her and reflexively, Caroline caught them. "I suggest you have a look and know what is being said." The dowager marchioness used her now-free hands to pat at her artfully arranged hair. "Now, you needn't worry. I will fix this."

Warning bells chimed away in her mind. She didn't want to know. Not knowing was preferable and yet, she proved a glutton for self-suffering. "What?"

"The Duke of Lennox is in need of a wife."

Her stomach churned. "His Grace?" As in her late father's good friend? "He is ancient," she blurted.

"Caroline," her mother chided. "Do not be rude. His Grace is recently widowed, and still heirless."

Heirless. Which meant he would want nothing more than to get a babe on her and—

I can't. "I cannot marry him." Even she was not that desperate.

The dowager marchioness's thin eyebrows arched. "Do you truly believe you can afford to be anything but grateful for *any* match you're able to make?" The casual deliverance of that query proved somehow more insulting than had it been shot out impatiently. "I've already spoken with him."

She'd already…

Caroline shook her head, not even realizing she'd done

so until her mother spoke.

"I have, and he is…amenable to the match. Though he would like to meet you again as it has been more than seven years since he's seen you, and he wishes to be sure you are agreeable to him."

"That *I* am agreeable to *him*?" she choked out.

"Well, he *is* a duke, and you *are* a spinster." With that, she spun in a whir of skirts, and marched off.

Caroline stared after her retreating frame. Had there ever been a mother with so little regard for her children? Giving her head a shake, she glanced down—and promptly wished she hadn't. The papers she'd been running from stared up mockingly.

"She's wrong, you know," a quiet voice called out, and Caroline looked up to find her young niece, Violet, on the stairs above, staring down.

"Violet," she said dumbly.

Oh, *no*. How much had the girl heard?

Violet skipped down the stairs. "I did hear it all, and I have it in good mind to tell my father. Father would not like what she said to you."

"Please do not," Caroline said on a rush. The last thing she wanted to do was create more tension in her brother's home.

Violet reached the bottom step. "Oh, you needn't worry. I'm very good at keeping secrets. I want to tell him. But I shan't."

She gave her niece a small, grateful smile. Her younger niece…that was, her niece who'd still not made her Come Out.

Even she likely will be wed before me. That is, if Caroline didn't agree to that match.

"Where are you going?" Violet asked, with the blunt

honesty only a child possessed.

"To Hyde Park."

"That is *vastly* better than being yelled at by Grandmere."

Caroline winked. "Indeed."

"May I accompany you?"

"You do not have to do that." She'd not make a young girl suffer through her company.

"But I *want* to." And with the way her niece placed that slight emphasis upon that particular word, it rather sounded like she wished to.

"I would like that very much," she said, her throat thick with emotion.

Violet beamed. "Splendid."

Caroline looked to Agatha. "Violet and Miss Wilson will be joining me today." Her maid deserved a reprieve.

The girl dipped a curtsy, and with a smile, she hurried off.

A short while later, Caroline, Violet, and Miss Wilson made their way to the park. As governess and charge discussed the rise of the Greek tyrants, Caroline stared out the window at the passing townhouses and considered the happy couples strolling the pavement.

The rub of it was, her mother was right. Caroline had no prospects. If she wanted to have a family, her options were…limited. And now that she'd come to know Wynn, even with an understanding he'd marry another, she found herself unable to stomach the prospect of joining herself with anyone else.

He on the other hand? He will marry Lady Beatrice and never give me another thought.

Everything inside hurt at the truth of that.

They arrived at Hyde Park. Caroline stepped down after her niece and followed behind at a leisurely pace.

If she were now being truthful with herself, that moment on the terrace when he'd cared for her injured leg hadn't been the first time she'd been aware of him. Nay, there'd been nothing coincidental about the fact that when he'd come calling on Lettie, Caroline was always there to collect the flowers he'd arrived with for her sister. She'd been so very pathetic, wanting to spend time with Wynn, she'd kept him company while he waited for the real woman he'd come to visit.

Their talks had been the usual pleasantries—the weather, those talks in turn morphing into a lamentation on the misery of English weather, and a talk of other places, far away that enjoyed greater sun and warmth. And in those chance exchanges, she'd found herself asking him of places he'd been, and would like to go. In those instances of asking, she'd known he'd ultimately travel with her sister.

And she continued to make a cake of herself over him now.

"Here we are Aunt Caro," Violet announced, gesturing to the area she'd led them.

Tucked away on the furthest edge of Hyde Park, deep within a copse so that they wouldn't be seen, it was perfect.

Snatching the blanket from Miss Wilson's fingers, Violet snapped the fabric open, and set it down.

Caroline joined governess and charge on the blanket and tipped her face up to the sun stealing through the leaves overhead. How good it felt. Why one could almost forget—

"Do you know what I think you should do, Aunt Caroline?"

Caroline shook her head. "What is that poppet?"

"I think you should take all those gossip pages, and just rip them up into a million tiny pieces and toss them out in the waters."

Caroline would need a million pairs of hands to manage the feat of destroying all the pages written about her these days. "That won't make what they're saying go away."

"No, but it will make you feel better, if just for a moment."

"I can read them for you, if you'd like?" Violet offered.

Caroline glanced down at her lap. "No. I can do it." She skimmed the first paragraph, and then promptly wished she hadn't. Caroline bit hard on the inside of her cheek, welcoming the pain for it blunted the sting of silent, but no less agonizing humiliation.

> *Given Lord E is in the market for a wife, Lady C's propensity for throwing herself in the gentleman's path undoubtedly makes sense. And yet, not even one so very desperate to wed should be desperate enough to ever dare court, and certainly not wed, the pitiable, the pathetic Lady C.*

"What do they say?" Violet asked hesitantly.

She shot her head up. "Nothing that matters," she said on a rush. And because she knew her niece would be determined, lied. "Merely that I'm not at all a good instructor when it comes to flying kites."

As if there were no greater affront, Violet let out an indignant gasp. Her eyes flashed. "How dare they?" The girl grabbed for the kite she'd brought along. "It is well known that you were instructing me, Elspeth, and Lord Exmoor the other day. Therefore, I must make myself seen flying this kite."

Leaning over, Caroline tweaked the end of her niece's nose. "I think flying your kite is a lovely idea, poppet." She'd not have the young girl hiding away here with her. She deserved to be off, playing freely.

Violet jumped to her feet. "Come along, Miss Wilson. We're going flying." The pair started on their way when Violet said something to the governess. The young woman waited while Violet bounded back over to Caroline.

She stared up at her niece. "What is it, Violet?"

"I just wanted to say…he really is not worth your time."

He, as in Wynn Masterson, the Marquess of Exmoor.

"Why, he doesn't even fly a kite that well," Violet said on a rush. "And he certainly can't climb trees."

So her niece had read those pages. She knew precisely what they were saying.

She inclined her head. "Thank you, Violet," she said softly.

"You'll see I'm right. There will be a gentleman for you. A worthy one. One who always catches you when you fall."

Caroline forced a smile she did not feel and stared after her niece as she raced off.

Caroline knew precisely what Wynn Masterson, the Marquess of Exmoor in fact, was. All society knew he'd been a devoted son and brother, traits absent from so many of the men who were either rogues or dandies and who always put their interests and pleasures before even the thought of their female kin.

Caroline thought Violet was wrong on any number of scores she'd spoken of so confidently. The second being the naïve, hopeful idea that Caroline would find a gentleman. Those assurances she'd been making to Caroline, for six long years now.

And lastly, Lord Wynn was certainly no bumbling fool, and he would never be unworthy. He was a gentleman who, despite being thrown over by Caroline's sister, continued to show her kindness. Kindness that he most certainly needn't have done. Particularly not as Lettie had tossed him over for another and made him a source of his own gossip.

And he was a gentleman who still accompanied his sister to the park and bantered with her and conversed freely with her…and…

It put her so much in mind of how loving and devoted her own brothers were.

Caroline returned her focus to the latest gossip.

The papers had grown meaner.

Nay, the papers were inanimate. They just contained words about the actions of others.

The *people* had grown meaner.

Their cuts crueler, and their cruel whisperings, gleeful.

What had she expected, however?

Staring unblinkingly at the pages of *The London Examiner*, Caroline took in the latest words written about her.

She'd thought there was no worse fate than being the ruined Brookfield sister.

She'd been wrong.

So very, very wrong.

She wanted to go back to the far simpler time when she'd first made her debut and her reputation had been intact and all possibilities had been endless.

But this?

A woman so desperate to wed that she continually hurled herself at the feet of a gentleman –the same gentleman who'd been thrown over by her sister—courting another, far more respectable lady……well, this was not to be born.

She—

Caroline felt him before she heard him.

Somehow, she'd become so very attuned to his presence.

And it surely spoke to just how pitiable she was that she longed for his company, still.

"You," Wynn exclaimed.

She waggled her fingers. "Me."

"I did not expect to find you in here."

Which meant had he known she was here, he'd not have ventured in. She hated the admission should hurt so. "It is fine," she returned, her tones tight to her own ears, and Lord forgive her, she was helpless to soften them. Caroline climbed to her feet.

His eyes flared. "Not that I would avoid this area because you were here."

And yet, how damningly quick that denial had come.

He cleared his throat. "That is, I *would* avoid it." She curled her toes sharply. "Not because of you. But because we should not be seen together," he finished weakly.

It was forbidden not only because they were alone without the benefit of a chaperone, but because there was another woman whom he'd wed; the flawless, golden-haired beauty whom he'd begun courting.

Caroline made herself speak. "Of course." He really should leave. Or her. One of them should.

If they were discovered here, she'd be ruined all over again, and he clearly regretted finding her here. Unlike she him.

So what defect of character did she possess, that even knowing all that, she couldn't compel herself to go?

He cleared his throat. "Not because I regret that we

keep...colliding."

And just like that, with his subtle jest, the tension broke. Her lips twitched up at the corners, and they shared a smile. Theirs was an intimate, private exchange. In every way.

He beat his palm against his leg softly; in a distracted little way; a restless one. But still, he did not again speak.

"You really are free to leave, my lord," she ventured hesitantly.

Did she imagine regret at that formal address she'd tacked on in place of the usual Christian name he'd allowed her freedom to use?

"I'd rather not," he spoke quietly, in hushed, more steady tones than before, and her heart quickened.

His gaze slid over her face, and then to her hair. "May I?" he said quietly, and she stared, incapable of words; unable to do anything beyond nod slightly giving ascent for whatever it was he wished.

And then he stretched out a hand, and her breath froze as he tenderly brushed the side of her head; his knuckles caressed her cheek, and the warmth of his gloveless fingers upon her skin brought her eyes briefly closed.

Wordlessly, he plucked the bits of brush from her hair, flicking them to the ground, and his was a purposeful task.

She realized as much.

He merely sought to remove the remnants of twigs and sticks and leaves from her hair, and yet neither her body nor mind cared for those details.

She'd known far greater intimacies with Dylan, and yet there was something different in this.

Wynn's touch was warm. Gentle.

He stopped, his eyes lingering on her face once more,

that piercing blue gaze meeting hers.

She dampened her lips. "B-better?" she asked, her voice emerging breathless and husky.

"Perfect," he murmured.

And her heart tripped another beat. For in this instance, it felt very much like he spoke about her.

He looked down and the moment was shattered. His gaze locked on the center page of *The London Examiner*.

And she cringed. tensing her hands into tight balls at her side.

He'd know she'd been sitting here mourning the loss of him. A loss that hadn't even been real because there'd never been anything between them. Not truly. Not beyond a few shared exchanges that had meant far more to her.

"What did they say in that one?"

She shot her head up to find those curiosity filled eyes upon her.

He nudged his chin at the papers.

So this was what her hesitation to leave had cost her.

The rest of her pride.

Caroline shook her head.

Then, Wynn knelt and helped himself to those pages.

She should have ripped them up as her niece had suggested. She should have torn them into a thousand pieces and set them out upon the waters, blurring the ink words and inevitably drowning the sheets.

The sheets that were now, instead, held within this man's hands.

He flicked his gaze swiftly over the column, his eyes moving quickly as he read. She tensed her hands at her sides, for watching him as close as she was, she knew by the sudden stiffening of his wiry frame the very moment his attention went from that first less than flattering article about her, to the damning, humiliating one about her attempts to steal his affections from Lady Beatrice.

Caroline glanced up at the canopy of crisp green leaves overhead; following their gentle sway, as a light breeze set them to dancing.

Please, do not say anything, she silently implored.

With a sound of disgust, he tossed it down.

Shame blazed hotly through her, and Caroline hurriedly gathered up the papers and held them close to her chest, daring him with her eyes to say something.

Most other gentleman—any other gentleman—would not address it.

He did square on.

"I am sorry they've cut their teeth on you," he said.

She blinked slowly.

That was the opinion he'd arrived at. Which meant, he hadn't deduced that this time she'd not given two thoughts about what they were saying about her. This time, she'd lamented what they were saying about him… him and Lady Beatrice.

Funny how this felt a good deal safer.

"It is not your fault," she said softly.

"Yes, well, if I'd swifter reflexes it would have helped some," he said dryly. "In fact, that is really what the stories should be; my shockingly poor catching skills."

And the realization of what he did; this self-deprecating show, disparaging himself so as to save her humiliation… Despite herself, for the first time since the Great Fall Witnessed Round the Ballroom, she found her lips turning up at the corners, and she found herself falling in love with him all over again.

He grinned; smiling with her and not about her, and

her heart filled with warmth.

He waggled an eyebrow. "Though, my sisters would have taken great delight in pointing out that I've hardly been adept in that area when we played games of cricket and now tree-climbing."

"Yes," she said dryly. "Well, I daresay it's a good deal different catching a ball than it is catching a grown woman."

They shared a smile.

"It's all rubbish, you know," he said quietly.

She stared confusedly back.

"The rot they'll print."

Her gaze slipped to the front page, and her eyes snagged upon the other headline, she shared a place with.

Him.

But was it untrue rot?

Given he'd danced two sets with the Duke of Somerset's sister, she rather thought not.

Caroline made a show of studying the story.

And it was a story.

A story about a man who continually found himself rejected by the ladies he courted, who invariably found themselves with another, and wonderings about whether this time, Lady Beatrice might in fact be the one to heal his broken heart.

Riiiiip.

She glanced over and widened her eyes.

Wynn stood with the paper rent in half, two ends in either of his hands.

"Do you know, Violet recommended I do that," she remarked.

Riiiiiip. He gave those sheets a second tear. "Your niece is wise." He ripped it again and held the torn newspaper out. "You really should give it a go."

Caroline hesitated, and then taking them, she proceeded to shred into it.

It gave with a satisfying rip, and it was as invigorating as when she'd been racing through Hyde Park, flying a kite with Wynn, but only in a different way. In a way that said she didn't give a damn about what they said about her. In a way that said the words printed on the pages by these people were naught and meant naught, and Caroline turned herself over to the task until smaller scraps slipped from her fingers.

Her chest heaving, she looked over and found Lord Wynn's gaze on her.

"I rather think you have the hang of it," he said solemnly, and then he grinned, and she found herself smiling in return.

And then, the remnants in hand, Caroline drew her arms back and heaved those pieces out; they rained upon the water; tiny scraps of black and white that were caught by the lake's gentle pull and drawn away.

Dropping his arms onto his narrow waist, Wynn followed the path they traveled.

Side by side, she and the marquess watched them float off together.

"Do you know," he marveled in contemplative tones, "I hadn't thought about drowning them, but that's a splendid merger. Make sure we kill it dead."

His words startled a laugh from her, and he joined in, the deep rumble of his mirth melding with hers. When was the last time anyone had laughed with her, or because of anything she'd done. She'd been so busy being serious, she didn't remember what it was to laugh. Freely, that was.

Not the practiced trill her mother had drilled into her that had somehow obliterated all real joy.

And it felt so very good.

And she could almost forget what the world said about her, or that the man beside her had in fact been in love with her sister.

Alas, the latter thought proved all too sobering.

"I am sorry," he said quietly.

And those were perhaps the worst words he could utter; those pitying ones.

And perhaps she was a braver woman than she'd ever credited herself as being, for somehow, Caroline found the willpower to meet his eyes. "It is fine," she offered that requisite reassurance. "It—" And then she abruptly stopped. Her gaze unblinking, she stared ahead her eyes locked on his snowy white cravat, and suddenly the truth exploded from her. "Do you know, it is not."

He cocked his head.

"It is a lot of rot. I'll have you know, I did not throw myself at your feet."

"No, I know that," he said with a rapidity and sureness that bespoke the truth of his concurrence.

But in this moment, however, it was not about him. It was as though, she'd been freed. And then the words came tumbling out, and she began to pace. "My mother is mercenary and yet, that is a secondary footnote to the daughter who was flung at some gentleman's feet." His feet. Her own steps grew more frenzied; dried leaves that had long ago surrendered their place to the forest floor, cracked and crunched as she walked. "They are always cruel. Not a thing favorable to say. Only anything unkind. And they twist everything to suit them." Without any care for the fact that the words splashed upon the gossip pages were about real people. And yet...it occurred to her. "It isn't just me," she murmured. He was as much a central part of the gossip.

"Ah, yes." Scooping up a handful of stones, Wynn tossed them one at a time in a distracted way at the serene surface of the lake. "I too am front and center. '*The Marquess who Couldn't Marry*,' I believe is the headline today?"

Nay. The actual title was, "*The Marquess who Couldn't Marry...Until Now*" Because the gossips well knew Lady Beatrice would not reject his suit. That didn't, however, diminish the fact that they still wrote cruel words about Wynn because he'd been tossed over two times before.

Each rejection had come in a most public way—on the heels of another couple's greatest happiness.

"I'm sorry," Caroline said quietly, because she was not the only one hurting.

He waved a hand, dismissing that apology. "Such is the way."

"Lettie loves the duke," she blurted.

He stiffened.

"Forgive me," she said on a rush. "That...what I meant to say..." Caroline grimaced. Blast, she was a blunderer where words were concerned. She tried again. "Did you love my sister?" she spoke with a boldness and bluntness her youngest sister would have been hard pressed to not admire her for.

Wynn's expression grew contemplative. "I...enjoyed your sister's company," he finally said, and that admission hit Caroline square in the heart. "She is someone who it is very easy to speak with."—*Unlike me*—"She is someone comfortable in herself."—*Unlike me*—"And she's someone who's not stiffly proper—*Why? Why did I start this questioning*? Oh, she knew, and yet, she wished she could recall it.—"But I did not love her."

Caroline's silent lamentations came to a screeching halt, and she jerked her gaze from the point beyond his shoulder and met his stare squarely.

His focus however, remained trained on the lake behind them.

"Did you believe you loved her?" she asked hesitantly.

"No." This time Wynn's answer came so quick, Caroline released a breath she'd not even realized she'd had trapped in her lungs.

"Love is not something afforded most members of the peerage."

"You don't believe in it?"

"On the contrary," he countered so quickly, there was no doubting his sincerity. "My parents were very much in love."

Unlike Caroline's parents who'd had a most perfunctory, formal arrangement, similar to the marriage Caroline's mother wished for her to make with the duke. It'd been why as an innocent girl she'd wished desperately to know that sentiment in her one-day future marriage and believed Lord Somerville's lies.

"I should expect having witnessed true love, that you should want that emotion for yourself," she spoke softly. And that he'd not settle for just a suitable, respectable match with Lady Beatrice.

Or…perhaps he does in fact care for the lady. *I don't really know him or his connection to her.* That thought cut through her like a knife.

"Have you ever seen a shooting star, Caroline?"

At that sudden shift in discourse, she cocked her head a moment, and then nodded.

"How many times?" he persisted with his unexpected

line of questioning.

"When I was a girl," she said wistfully. "My sister and brother and I, we would sneak outside on summer days, and there was this enormous hill." The same hill she and her siblings would lie upon and roll down until their laughter was as dizzy as their heads from all the spinning. "At night, we'd find the highest spot, and lie shoulder to shoulder and just look up at the sky; it was filled with so many stars. There were so many flickers of light." Unlike London with its fog and dirt that had stolen the stars' placement in those heavens. "We would look for shooting stars to make a wish upon."

He slid closer. "And how many did you see?" he prodded.

A breeze wafted through the copse of trees, stirring the branches overhead; the light gust caught an errant curl that had been artfully arranged by her maid—because every part of Caroline these days was contrived. Suddenly, sad by the realization of all the ways in which she'd changed, she found herself unable to speak through the lump in her throat. She made herself lift a finger. "One."

"Just because you haven't found love, doesn't mean you should settle. You should have someone who wants to be with you, as you deserve."

SHE SPOKE SO FREELY OF love, about Wynn finding it for himself, and even as he knew that wasn't an option, in this instant, it wasn't himself he thought of. He didn't want to speak about what his future dictated.

Rather, he was consumed by thoughts of Caroline and the past he knew nothing of. There could be no doubting she spoke about that sentiment with a surety only afforded one who'd herself been in love.

And alternately, Wynn both wanted to know, and never have confirmation of his suspicions, because something about thinking of her in love with another man, stirred a primal, seething jealousy he'd never before known. Not when he'd attempted to court Lady Daisy, and never when he'd courted Caroline's own sister.

Wynn balled his hands and unballed them. Over and over. That virulent feeling didn't dissipate. Rather, it threatened to devour him whole.

And then the weight of not knowing about her and the pain she carried was too much. It was greater than even his own desire to not know.

Wynn took a step closer. "You were in love?"

Caroline dampened her lips and for a moment he thought she'd leave him with only an unanswered question, and then she nodded slowly. "Yes." And she spoke softly.

He'd been expecting it, but even having that supposition confirmed with her short utterance unleashed more of that stinging heat inside his chest.

Then it was as though in answering that truth aloud freed her. "I was young. I'd just made my debut. He was…exciting."

Her gaze grew distant, and he knew the moment she was recalling that other man, and Wynn wanted to climb inside her memory, pummel the blackguard, and steal a future for Wynn and Caroline, one that wasn't riddled by the woes that had ultimately found them.

She smiled softly. "Unlike other gentleman, his hair was too long, and his cravat was always rumpled."

Unbidden, Wynn stole an awkward peek down at his

perfectly tied knot.

"It was entirely respectable at first. He claimed his two sets...and would never dance with another. All the while I had other partners, he would just watch as though I was the only woman in the room." She spoke with the wonderment of someone who all these years later could not fathom that anyone would feel that way about her.

And yet, I am right here. Now that I've seen her, she is the only woman I think of.

Not Beatrice. Not the lady he needed to marry.

"He was charming, made me laugh, and always wore a smile himself."

With every word she spoke, jealousy continued to nip at every corner of his soul, chipping and chiseling away.

"He painted an image of both the future and a marriage I yearned for."

"And his intentions were dishonorable," he said, already knowing. Because had they not been, she would have been happily married and Wynn wouldn't be standing alone here with her now.

Her eyes grew sad. "I gave myself to him believing we would marry. He was pockets to let and though I knew as much, never did I believe his courtship of me was because of my dowry, and that when my brother vowed he'd not see a penny of it, he'd throw the fact that I'd given him my virginity in Miles's face."

"Oh, Caroline," he whispered, wanting to take her in his arms, and then hunt down the blackguard.

"Nor did I expect that he'd just..." She stretched her fingers towards the trail leading out of the copse. "Walk away." Caroline let her arm fall to her side.

It was a certainty the man had never deserved her, and Wynn would wager his soul that he was one with whom he had no dealings because he didn't know a man who wouldn't have the sense to have protected Caroline's heart the way it should have been.

"Who?" Wynn seethed, needing a name so that he could pummel the bastard when next they met.

She cocked her head.

"Who was he?"

"Does it matter?" she countered.

Yes, was the unequivocal answer that sprung to his lips born of a truth he did not understand. "I suppose not."

Caroline rested her back against the trunk of a narrow oak, casual in her repose, when there was nothing casual about the words she spoke. "The Earl of Somerville."

Somerville.

A notorious rake. He and the earl had never traveled in the same circles but even Wynn had heard of the other man's proclivities for the gaming tables.

Wynn moved closer, stopping just a pace away from where she lounged. A breeze tugged at a loose curl arranged at her shoulder. "I should think you'd be more..." Only close as he was, he caught the raspberry fragrance that clung to her skin, faint and yet entrancing.

"Cynical?" she supplied, wholly unaware of the havoc wrought by their nearness. "Because one man betrayed me?" She scoffed. "I'm not so small-minded as to judge the actions of all men because one of them hurt me. I've seen my brothers fall in love and marry. I've seen the wonderful husbands and fathers they are. I know love is real and exists." Her lips pulled again in a sad rendering of a smile. "Just...not for every woman."

Of its own volition, Wynn's hand came up, and he teased a finger along the corner of her mouth.

Her breath caught.

"Caroline," he whispered, hoarsely, wanting her to order him gone, because that was all that kept him from kissing her as he hungered to.

Caroline's long, inky black lashes fluttered, and she tipped her mouth up towards his. "Wynn," she breathed; his name an invitation and capitulation, and he surrendered himself to both.

Even as their lips met, he cupped her nape, and her hands came up to twined about his neck. Wynn angled her chin, deepening the kiss.

The rasps of their roughened breathing melded with the rustle of leaves dancing overhead.

She moaned; parting, she let him in, and Wynn tasted of her. She drank of him in return, boldly caressing her tongue against his.

Fire burned between them as their embrace took on a touch of desperation. A kiss would never be enough. He wanted—

"Aunt Carooooo!"

With a gasp, he and Caroline wrenched apart.

All the color fled her cheeks. "I should—"

"Yes," he said quickly, as tucking tendrils that had fallen loose from her arrangement back behind her ears.

"Do I look all right?" she whispered.

Magnificent. Glorious. "Fine," he made himself say, his voice thickened still with yearning for her.

Caroline's eyes darkened, and she swayed towards him, once more.

"Aunt Carrrro?"

That second call, this time closer, stole the rest of their interlude.

Gathering up the hem of her skirts, Caroline dashed off.

Wynn stared after her as she took flight. There should be relief at having not been discovered in a compromising position. There should be dread at how close he'd come to being found alone with Caroline.

And yet there wasn't.

There was just this agony of regret and a keen sense of loss at having finally come so very close to the exact someone he wanted, but without hope of anything more with her.

CHAPTER 13

THE PAPERS CONTINUED TO WRITE about Caroline.

This time, however, she didn't care what the papers said about her. This time, she bypassed her name and found that of another. And because she was a glutton for pain, she'd closeted herself away in the same parlor Wynn had used to visit Lettie and read the latest headline.

Lord E and Lady B

Is there a more respectable pairing than the eminently respectable marquess to the Duke of S's sister. Such a perfect match, it is a wonder this person failed to see that most obvious of connections.

Why, with the Curse of a Duke upon him, it only makes sense that marriage to the daughter—now the sister—of a duke should be that which breaks Lord E's auspicious streak of losing the ladies he courts to the handful of dukes in London.

Lady B who is several years past the bloom of her first youth, but who remains lovely and respectable and as a mature woman, a splendid option for—

Caroline's heart seized up, and she wrenched her gaze away from the rest of the lengthy praise heaped upon the Duke of Somerset's sister. That lady who Wynn would wed. And yet, of all the splendid attributes the papers wrote of, the singularly hardest one to read was—respectable.

For it was something Caroline hadn't been in so long.

It was why the men of Polite Society had deemed her unworthy.

It was why she remained unwed with the only prospect before her, marriage to the Duke of Lennox.

She knew what this news meant. Her mother would be relentless in her determination to see Caroline marry the Duke of Lennox. That was the expectation her mother had for her.

Of course, Caroline, wasn't naïve. She knew the duke was her only option and that she was set to face an empty marriage to a doddering lord, and really the misery of that should be the only one that she confronted this morning.

Caroline sucked in a shuddery breath.

Only it wasn't.

Unbidden, her gaze slipped back to those hated pages.

"You silly, stupid girl," her mother raged.

Startled, Caroline jerked her head up.

The dowager marchioness stormed into the room, waving about a copy of the very paper Caroline now read. Oh, dear. Angry footsteps and a raised voice. This was not good.

"Good morning, Moth—"

"It most certainly is not a good morning," she snapped. "That is unless you consider the fact that everyone in London is speaking about how you continue to throw yourself at a man who's all but betrothed to Lady Beatrice Dennington."

It seemed she was destined to have this same discussion with her mother, *every blasted morning*.

Rage mingled with envy, twisting unpleasantly in her gut. "I've not thrown myself at him," she said, with a calm she didn't know how she managed. "You did."

"I did it once, and you continued. And now, this?" Her mother hurled the pages onto the table before Caroline.

She glanced down.

> *The Duke of Lennox, once rumored to be interested in a match with the pitiably desperate Lady Caroline B appears to have shifted his attentions to **another** Lady Caroline. This one would do well to not make the same mistake as made by another, more scandalous, Caroline...*

Ahh, so this was the true source of the dowager's rage.

The duke had begun courting another. *Another* poor Caroline. This one notoriously impoverished, with a spendthrift brother, and as few prospects as Caroline herself. She should feel only relieved, and yet sadness for that other young woman filled her, too.

"Do you have nothing to say?" her mother demanded, and Caroline looked up.

"Apparently any Caroline will do," she muttered, ringing a gasp from her mother's lips.

"You would dare make light? You won't be so smug when he marries her...or...or...someone else who isn't you."

"Relieved," she said, and it was harder to say who was more stunned by that challenge, her or the dowager whose jaw slackened, and eyes flared. "Not smug. *Relieved*."

Splotches of color splashed her mother's cheeks. "Relieved? And why, exactly? Because you flew a kite with Lord Exmoor and his youngest sister?"

She winced.

Only, her mother was not done. "You were so desperate for his affections, you actually launched yourself at him."

This was really enough. Caroline stormed to her feet. "This from the same person who pushed me at Lord Exmoor. Literally and figuratively."

"That was before he dropped you," her mother said between tightly clenched teeth.

"Are you truly suggesting he'd fail to catch me because he'd send a message to society?" she asked incredulously. Her mother knew Wynn not at all if she believed him so very mercenary in his thinking.

"I'm saying just that. It was a testament to how little he saw you, and how little interest he had or will ever have in you." Every casually flung word from her mother was an arrow that found a mark in Caroline's heart. "You will not let me coordinate a marriage between you and the duke, and for what? Hmm?" Her mother was a dog with a bone. "The marquess who now finds himself with a lady of a stellar reputation and sterling background? A woman who is your superior in every way?" Her mother nudged her chin at the newspaper.

Unbidden, Caroline found her gaze drawn there and

promptly wished she hadn't.

She wished she'd looked anywhere other than the paper she now did—or more specifically, about the couple she now read of.

Wynn and—

"Lady Beatrice, the Duchess of Somerset's sister," her mother murmured.

Near in age to Caroline, Lady Beatrice was a woman who also found herself unwed.

That, however, was where all other similarities ended.

Exceedingly.

That was the word Caroline had mustered in her mind for Lady Beatrice.

With pale golden perfectly coiled ringlets and pleasing face and figure, Lady Beatrice was *exceedingly* lovely.

As her mother had pointed out, Lady Beatrice also possessed an impeccable reputation, and came from an exceedingly powerful family. Even as the lady's brother had married the sister of a notorious gaming hell owner, that union had only cemented their family's position of power and influence.

And the lady was also an exceedingly graceful dancer, a factor Caroline hadn't noted before, for the simple reason there'd been no reason to note as much—until now.

Until she'd read about Wynn having partnered the lady for two sets. Two waltzes, at that.

And never had Caroline felt more like curling up and crying which, given the fact she'd been both deceived and ruined by her first love, was saying a good deal, indeed.

She'd allowed herself to believe…

What? a niggling voice whispered. *Did you believe that latest meeting with him in Hyde Park yesterday had somehow changed something—anything—between you? That you've been* *something **more** to him?*

Only, that was precisely what it had been to her.

As her mother lit into her with a lecture about the sad, sorry future that awaited her, Caroline forced her gaze away from the pairing of Wynn's name and another woman's on those pages, making herself look anywhere that was not there.

Her mother was not wrong.

Caroline could not admit, if even to herself, that she'd been secretly longing for…more. More with Wynn.

She saw that now.

She also at last made herself see the futility of it.

There was no future with Wynn.

And suddenly, she made herself confront the only real future that awaited her—one as the spinster aunt, sister, and daughter, continually reminded of all her greatest failings by this woman before her.

She didn't want that, any more than she wanted to find herself an object of pity by her always generous siblings and their families.

Nay, she knew what she needed to do.

"Caroline? Caroline?" her mother demanded. "Are you listening to me?"

"Of course, I am, Mother," she said, her voice hollow to her own ears. "You are right."

The dowager drew back; her eyes flared wide.

And before she lost the courage, Caroline made herself complete the words. "I will…not discourage the duke's suit." There that was as close as she could to promising she'd marry him.

Her mother smiled.

Her mother never smiled, and yet, this time, Caroline's capitulation had managed to elicit that rare expression. It was really the first Caroline could ever recall the dowager marchioness having been proud of her or any of her children for that matter. That happy quirk of her lips was gone as quickly as it had come.

"That is the wise decision." She gave a toss of her head. "Now, you must hope that the duke is still interested in marriage to you. I will pay him a visit this morn and see what I may do to revive the match." With that, her mother stalked off with determined steps.

Caroline stared after her, and then reached down, not for the paper with the name of her future husband front and center, but of another.

She closed her eyes.

It was decided.

So why did she feel so very miserable?

CHAPTER 14

Wynn had always been practical and logical. He'd never acted on emotion, and he'd never been impulsive. And he'd certainly, absolutely, never done something so outrageous as to disregard what was best for his sisters and pursue his own self-interests and passions.

Never more, however, had he regretted being the honorable brother who put other people—his family's—interests before his own.

Later that week, Wynn stood on the sidelines of Lord and Lady Stanhope's ballroom with his mother quietly going over her expectations for him that evening. As she continued her hushed prattling, he found his gaze locked on the entrance, searching for a sight of her.

Just as he'd been searching for her since their last meeting.

Not the woman his mother wished for him to wed.

Not the lady who with her connections would make him the most respectable match.

But rather Caroline. He wanted to see *her* and speak

with her. Because he found himself enjoying her company as he'd never enjoyed another woman's.

Speaking with her was easy when it hadn't been natural with any woman before her. That was, any woman to whom he wasn't related.

Had he ever waited on the sidelines of a dance floor, awaiting with this same eagerness the arrival of Lady Lettie or Lady Daisy, both of whom he'd had previous intentions of marrying? He could say definitively he did not.

He'd liked them enough.

They were kind and comfortable women to be around, but there'd not been this sense of anticipation.

"...quite lovely, is it, not?" his mother was saying.

And never had he felt with another woman the passion he had known with Caroline. "Quite," he murmured.

There'd been something electric between them.

"Mmm hmm." He offered that noncommittal response to whatever it was his mother now said.

Caroline had kissed with a wild abandon with a spirited passion that defied the impressively measured woman Polite Society saw.

"...of course, I'll require your approval."

"You have it," he said absently to whatever it was his mother was speaking about.

"...because it isn't every day a lady sets out to tour the Continent on her own."

Caroline was—

Wynn blinked slowly and glanced down at his mother.

Her eyes twinkled. "Wynn, have you even heard one word I'm saying?" she asked gently.

"I have." The lie came easy. Anything to end her haranguing.

Reminiscent of the way she'd done when he'd been a boy, the dowager marchioness gathered him gently by the elbow. "I was noting that Lady Beatrice is yet to arrive."

"Yes, I…realize that."

Actually, he hadn't.

He'd been so lost in thought, wondering about the presence of another—of Caroline. "I'm sure she'll be here soon." That didn't bring the joy and excitement it should.

His mother considered him for a long moment. "You have not paid the lady a visit since Monday."

No, he'd not. After his latest meeting with Caroline, he'd been unable to bring himself to call on another.

In the end, he was saved by the arrival of Alice as the latest set concluded, and her dance partner escorted her over. "What are we discussing?"

"Noth—"

"The fact that your brother did not call on Lady Beatrice since Monday," their mother whispered.

Alas, perhaps saved was the wrong choice of words, after all.

"I was busy," he gritted out.

They stared at him expectantly.

Folding his arms over his chest, Wynn stared mutinously out at the dance floor.

His mother's friend, Lady Donahue, joined them at last, granting Wynn a true reprieve. They exchanged polite greetings before the viscountess commanded the attention of Wynn's mother.

He stole another look around the room. Perhaps Caroline and her family were attending another event? What was she doing even now? Was she—?

"Looking for Lady Beatrice?" his sister whispered near soundlessly.

He blinked slowly, and then glanced down at his tenacious sister. "Yes," he lied.

"Liar." Alice pinched him lightly on the arm. "You are looking for someone." She paused. "But why do I suspect it is not the one society expects you're looking for?"

Wynn tensed; all the while, he made a show of observing the dancers in the midst of their latest set.

Alas, he should have trusted not engaging in the discussion about his distracted state would not deter her.

"I never thought to see you this way," his sister whispered, dabbing at the corners of her eyes.

"What way?" he said gruffly.

"In love."

He stilled.

That was the opinion his sister had reached? His mind balked. Yes, he enjoyed Caroline's company and spoke more easily with her than he'd ever any other woman, and he'd hungered for her since the moment he'd had her in his arms for that heated embrace. But…love?

It couldn't be. It—

His sister smiled widely and gave her brows a slight waggle. "You'll not even deny it."

Wynn's neck went hot. "You are making more out of it than there is."

For even as there could be more between him and Caroline, Wynn didn't have the luxury of following where his heart wished. As such, it was far better to not let his mind think of what could have been, and what never would be with the lady.

His sister's smile only grew wider. "I thought so." She sounded entirely smug and delighted, and he'd a sudden desire to slip off because he didn't want to discuss this with her, of all people.

To Marry Her Marquess

Suddenly, her triumphant grin slipped.

"You've always been the most dutiful brother and son."—*Not dutiful enough. Not when I've failed to pay attention when a bounder had been set on ruining her.* They were words he couldn't speak to his sister, and certainly not here.—"All those years ago, I knew you were courting and intending to marry Lady Daisy because you were fulfilling our parents' expectations for you."—*Yes, that much had been true.*— His sister shifted closer, and lowered her voice another fraction. "Just as I knew the reason for your sudden courtship of Lady Lettie." She lifted sad eyes to his. "And I hated that, because you are the best of brothers and best of men, and I've only ever wanted to see you happily married and in love."

His gut twisted.

How he hated this growing sense of guilt.

His mother touched a hand to his arm, saving Wynn from having to respond to Alice's regret-tinged words.

"She is here."

Anticipation built swiftly in his chest, as he swiftly followed his mother's discreet gesturing to the front of the room before realizing belatedly...she'd of course not been speaking about the same woman he and Alice had been discussing.

He followed her gaze to the young woman in question. Lady Beatrice entered with all the regal bearing only a duke's daughter might manage. Sandwiched between her brother and his wife, the lady passed bored eyes over the ballroom, looking as pained to be here as Wynn himself.

Panic built inside. The lady didn't have any romantic interest in him. In fact, with the way she avoided his gaze and him in general, it was doubtful she even liked him.

Having had more Seasons than most ladies and remaining

unmarried through the lot of them, Lady Beatrice was a good deal more mature in years and temperament than most other women present. She was unfailingly polite and, judging from the annual musicale her mother hosted to showcase the lady, possessed of a pleasing voice. And most importantly, with her connections to a duke and an in-law to men who ruled the underworld, she hailed from a family the Ton would never dare cut. That was... *again*. They'd attempted that feat years earlier, and it had only strengthened their position of power within society.

Lady Beatrice would make him a fine match: respectable, companionable. Safe. Strangely, Wynn had come to find the last thing he wanted in a marriage was the safe one.

Alas, safety was something his unmarried sisters were in desperate need of.

Just then, a noticeable charge filled the air.

Wynn froze, sensing her arrival.

It was as if he'd conjured her of his own wishing.

Caroline.

And then she and her mother were there. At the front of the receiving line.

He dismissed the mercenary mother outright, locking his gaze on the one who commanded his interest.

As did everyone else in the room; those whispers which hummed like a thousand angry bees. All eyes were upon her; many of them unkind, most of them pitying.

And he'd hand it to the lady; she had greater strength than most.

For she lifted her chin a fraction and brought her shoulders back with the regal bearing of a queen amidst her lowly subjects and stared straight on. The glow of the chandeliers highlighted the gleam of midnight tresses drawn elegantly back and held in place with a pair of ruby and diamond heart-shaped combs that paired perfectly with a more simple gold heart pendant that hung about her long neck.

And he found himself drinking in the sight of her; seeing her for the first time; the pale blue satin clung to her narrow hips and trim waist while the lace adornment along the bodice of her gown drew a man's eyes—drew *his* eyes—to generous breasts, lush and meant to fill a man's palms.

How had he failed to note her beauty before this Season?

How had he failed to see her years earlier? What would life have been had he noticed her long ago, and courted her instead, and then there'd never have been a bounder who'd ruined her.

She and her mother stopped on the sidelines of the dance floor, Caroline's eyes did a sweep of the room, and then her focus found him. Her gaze locked with his.

And he stilled as a small, playful smile formed on her full lips.

It was a secretive smile. An intimate one that he returned, all too easily, his own lips tipping up at the corners as they were united in this secret only they shared.

Alice brought him whirring back to the moment. "I need air. Walk with me, brother." Hers wasn't a question. Rather, she slipped her arm through his, and steered them away.

The moment they'd started on a turn around the ballroom, his sister spoke. "I daresay, in all the weeks in which you courted the lady's sister, I never saw you look upon her once the way you do Lady Caroline now." That quiet, slightly bemused murmuring brought him back, and Wynn pulled his gaze away from Caroline and looked to his sister.

Alice stared at him with all the knowing only a mischievous sister could be capable of.

"Oh, do not look so dumbstruck," she chided, rapping him lightly on the arm with her fan. "Do you think a sister does not notice these things?" She dropped her voice. "Granted, I believed it was just a manner of gossip. That Elspeth had struck up an unlikely friendship with the lady's sister, and you were merely drawn into that exchange. But seeing you now…" Tears pricked her eyes, and with her spare hand she dabbed at the corners. "It has always been my hope that you would find someone who should bring you the joy our parents had with one another. That you'd find yourself enrapt."

And not for the first time where his sister was concerned, there came a wave of guilt. He didn't have the luxury of following his heart. It was a truth he couldn't admit to her, not when she was largely the reason behind his obligations. Discomfited, Wynn shifted back and forth on his feet. "You are making much out of nothing."

His sister's frown deepened. "You didn't once fly a kite in Hyde Park with her?"

The gossips and the newspapers continued to wreak havoc on his existence. "I did," he said, as they continued their stroll. "But…her niece and Elspeth were also present."

"And have you not been watching the doorway for the lady's arrival for the better part of the evening?" she pressed, far too astute for his good.

Let him pray, however, that she wasn't that astute as to know just how much he regretted her circumstances that found him in his current straits.

His sister led him onward, keeping them to the outer

edge of the ballroom, squiring him away from those ladies who still believed he was some talisman for their landing a duke.

"I will not lie," she murmured, keeping her voice low enough so that her words were reserved for his. "I found Lady Lettie an agreeable match. Not necessarily the one I would have chosen for you, as she did not inspire a grand passion in you. However, she was polite and certainly friendly and ready with a smile, but I was not crushed for you when she wed another."

He found himself glancing to where Caroline stood, anchored between her dour-faced, pinch-mouthed mother and—

His eyes narrowed on the white-haired Duke of Lennox, sixty-five if he was a day, eying her bosom with entirely too much interest.

The ancient letch, certainly old enough to be her father, ogled her breasts.

Wynn balled his hands into tight fists.

The duke raised a monocle to his eye, and leaned in, peering lasciviously—

A growl climbed up his throat, and he had a sudden urge to do even more sudden violence to the old bastard, ancient or not.

"And that is precisely what I am talking about," his sister crowed triumphantly.

"What?" he gritted out.

Dead. He'd be happy to see the old duke dead for the way he leered at her like a starving man who'd found the only hope of sustenance trussed up in a blue gown before him.

His sister smirked. "You look like you wish to murder the Duke of Lennox. Which would be, of course, no less than the notorious letch deserves." The gloating smile left Alice's face, and she lowered her voice a tad, once more. "He's gone through four wives, each of them dying in the quest of giving him an heir. Given everything the gossip pages say about the Dowager Marchioness of Guilford, she is certainly scheming to put her daughter with that one."

Something volatile and raw and primal snaked through Wynn's veins; the red-hot sentiment coursing through him.

His sister leaned up and whispered. "Do go on. I shall not waste your time gloating. Go. Visit the lady and save her from those two." She paused. Her entirely too astute gaze narrowing and sharpening on his face. "That is, unless I am wrong?"

He wasn't intending to court Caroline. Because he couldn't.

It was reason enough to ignore his sister's urgings. "Go, then." She hit him again with her fan. "On with you."

Wynn's gaze slid back to Caroline and the duke.

Narrowing his eyes, Wynn quit his sister's side.

With every step that brought him closer to her, he became aware of the crowd's focus on him, and then the frenzy of whispers as he headed across the room. His eyes remained fixed on Caroline and Lennox.

Desperation wreathed Caroline's heart shaped features as she searched the crowd.

For Wynn?

Don't be ridiculous. The lady merely sought an escape from the duke reaching those long, gnarled fingers her way. That made the most sense.

Squaring his jaw, Wynn lengthened his stride; evading matchmaking mamas, his eyes for just one.

Wynn converged upon the trio and Caroline's eyes filled. Never had any woman—nay, any person—looked upon him the way this woman now did.

"Lady Guilford, Lady Caroline," he greeted, dropping a bow, and Caroline immediately drew her hand back and out of reach of the duke who, at Wynn's unexpected arrival, had been startled into loosening his hold.

The dowager marchioness smiled tightly. "Lord Exmoor. A pleasure, as always." Her tone conveyed anything but.

"Exmoor," the duke boomed, his voice elevated to an obscene level, a product of his failing hearing.

Ignoring that greeting, Wynn spoke to the dowager marchioness, even as his gaze remained locked with Caroline's. "I have come to request Lady Caroline's next set."

Caroline's brows lifted slightly.

"Caroline is to partner His Grace," the dowager marchioness said impatiently. The lady's let-down ended on a gasp, as he stretched a hand towards Caroline and so very naturally, she slipped her fingers into his, allowing him to maneuver her away from the pair.

They started for the dance floor.

"A rude one, he is," Lennox spoke loudly. "Knew his father in my day, and I can say, he would have never conducted himself so."

No, Wynn's father had never stirred a scandal. And until recently, neither had Wynn. As the whispers became a roar, he expected he should feel discomfited at finding himself the subject of focus.

And yet, he couldn't muster the energy to care.

"...you must forgive..." Caroline's mother was saying. "...she is quite sought after..."

Caroline gave an exaggerated roll of her eyes, and as Wynn and she took their place among the other dancers, they shared that smile; a private secret; he and she, two players in a secret production only they knew of.

CHAPTER 15

He'd saved her.

Two times now.

Both in ways far greater than she had a right to ask.

But he had.

Caroline had never before been saved.

She wasn't a lady men saved, let alone, for that matter, noted.

Case in point being his previous courtship of her sister, then her collapse at his feet when her mother had shoved her at him days ago.

Only to now find herself with Wynn as her partner in crime, and her salvation this Season and this night.

"I cannot thank you enough," she muttered; scarcely daring to move her lips, as with the way the crowd now watched her, they would certainly decipher every word she spoke.

"Come, you don't wish to have your toes trampled on by the Dying Duke," he said, teasingly, drawing a smile from her. "Your mother, however, seems all too eager to sacrifice your feet." He settled his large, heavy palm at her waist.

She trembled, certain he felt that shake roll through her at the feel and heat of him.

She reminded her brain to remind her mouth and tongue to move; to form words. "My mother is all too eager to sacrifice me to Satan if he showed up with flowers and a promise of marriage." As soon as the muttering left her mouth, she knew she should wish to call it back; that she should feel some modicum of embarrassment that she'd spoken so freely about her circumstances. And yet, oddly, all she felt was freed.

Wynn tensed; his palm curling sharply; his fingers biting briefly, uncomfortably into her side. "Surely she'd not see you wed Lennox?" he asked tersely, and she shivered.

In all the exchanges she'd had with him; from the hothouse to their meetings in the park to their daily exchanges when he'd courted her sister, never had she known him to display this volatile rage; the kind that thrummed under the surface.

She weighed her words. "My mother would see me wed anyone at this point," she explained, as he guided her through the steps of the waltz; steering her in long, smooth, looping circles.

"He is a reprobate and a lech—"

"And he's also the greatest,"—*as in the only*—"option for me, at this point," she said matter-of-factly.

His grip tightened once more upon her, and as soon as his fingers curled, he lightened that grip. "But you will not marry one such as him," he said flatly, his words not a question. "Right?" he added, forcing her to answer that question she didn't want to.

Suddenly, the implications of what he was asking

registered. He was, of course, only concerned that she might make a match with a duke and further fuel speculation. "Is this why you've danced with me, then?" she asked, unable to keep the hurt from her voice. "To lecture me on who I might marry?"

"I am not lecturing you," he said, his cheeks flushed. "I am trying to talk sense into you."

It did not, however, escape her notice that he didn't deny her charge; and her heart ached with that realization.

"Talk sense into me? I'm a grown woman, Wynn," she said quietly, lowering her voice, and meeting his stare directly. "I certainly don't require you to give me advice on my marital prospects or options."

He gripped her more forcefully, pulling her closer. "It appears someone should."

Her body trembled under the heat of his touch. "And you took that onerous responsibility on for yourself?" Caroline's retort emerged more than faintly breathless.

"It is not onerous."

But it *was* a responsibility. *She* was. Just like that, she went cold as those butterflies dancing in her belly froze and then died. "Poor Wynn," she said sadly.

He frowned. "What are you—?"

"How exhausting it must be for you," she went on. "Being above reproach and possessed of this great sense of responsibility for everyone." She paused, holding his eyes. "Do you ever even think about what you want?"

Yes, all the time. *Her.*

His gaze remained fixed on a point over the top of her head. "I don't have that luxury, Caroline." Because of that secret surrounding his family.

She chuckled; the sound quiet and low and devoid of humor.

He glanced at her, his frown deepening. "What is it?"

"It is, just you speak so loftily of what you must do. You will marry—to what gain? Improve your family's already stellar reputation? To increase your social standing?"

"You don't understand anything of it," he said, on a furious whisper; his hands tightening at her waist before he relaxed them.

"No, Wynn," she said calmly. "I rather believe it is you who don't understand anything. I'm not a young girl. I'm not some naïve, optimistic debutante who believes there is love right around the corner. Title or not, what lady would wish to marry one such as Lennox?" Why, when a gentleman like Wynn was right there before them. "And yet…what is the alternative? That I become a poor relation, dependent upon the kindness and generosity of her brothers?"

"They would not care for you?" His eyes flashed with outrage, and her heart trembled that he should feel that outrage on her behalf.

"They absolutely would," she assured him. "But if our roles were reversed, would you want to be living the rest of your days off your sisters' generosity?" She shook her head. "I don't think you would."

Wynn drew her closer, angling her body nearer and her heart quickened. "You deserve more than settling for the last best option, Caroline," he said, the fury in his whispered tones, somehow more tender and warmer than any endearment he might have proffered.

She felt beset by the need to cry, and she didn't want to. She didn't want to blubber in the middle of the dance floor. But more than that, she didn't want her miserable future intruding on this magical moment. "What are my other options, Wynn? Tell me?" she entreated. Certainly

To Marry Her Marquess

not him. Even as she wished it could be him.

The set came to an end; and even as she mourned that separation, she welcomed the end of his questioning.

The moment Wynn returned her to her mother's side, without a word, he dropped a bow and stalked off.

Caroline stared after his retreating figure; alternately wishing to call him back, and never wanting to see him again. Because he was not braver. Because he could kiss her and speak freely with her and laugh with her, while remaining committed to marrying another woman.

Her mother grabbed her lightly by the wrist. "I hope you are happy," she whispered furiously.

She wasn't. She was miserable.

"You rebuffed the duke's invitation to dance for a gentleman who is known to be seriously courting another. And the duke danced with *other* Caroline." Her nostrils flared. "Do not make that mistake again. He's escorted her back to her brother and is now coming this way."

With dread slithering in her belly, she looked across the ballroom. Sure enough, the Duke of Lennox made his way in Caroline's direction.

Tall, his back slightly bent, and the cane in his hand not merely an affected prop used by so many gentlemen, the duke limped his way down the stairs. Slowly. He moved very slowly; a man, just one strong gust of wind from being knocked over.

This is who her mother would have her marry. This ancient lord who'd had a bevy of wives before her and who would also overlook Caroline's scandal.

When not even an honorable man like Wynn Masterson, the Marquess of Exmoor would.

The irony wasn't lost on Caroline. She'd land herself a duke, and Wynn would land himself a duke's perfect sister. Only one of them, however, would have a miserable marriage, and it certainly was not the latter.

The duke was the best Caroline could hope for.

How dare Wynn dance with her this evening, with the express intent—with the *only* intent—of questioning her about the duke. As if Caroline had options. As if she could afford to simply ignore the only offer she'd received—ever—and likely ever would.

It was a match she knew her brother would never require her to make, and yet what options did she possess? What future awaited her, other than the one her mother had spoken so very truthfully of—that of poor, spinster aunt, reliant upon her generous brother and his equally generous family.

It was the only option she had.

With every limp that brought the duke closer; panic built in her breast, threatening to suffocate her.

She could not do this.

She did not want to do this.

Turning on her heel, Caroline bolted.

Her mother gasped. "Caroline. Where do you think you are—?"

The pounding of her heart combined with the din of the crowd drowned out the remainder of that question.

Caroline weaved between guests with only one goal driving her flight—freedom. The garish smiles and tittering laughter were distorted in her mind.

Not slowing her stride, she raced down a hallway, and through the doorways until she broke through the other side, to a place of quiet—her host's terrace where the air was cooler, and she took great, big gasps of air; letting it fill her lungs.

Caroline continued running; down the steps to the

gardens below, only stopping when the high brick wall met her, ending her flight.

Her chest heaving, she stared blankly at the cherry red bricks.

Trapped.

In every way.

CAROLINE DIDN'T WISH TO SEE him.

Why would she?

Their exchange on the dance floor had been tense and angry.

Yes, it was best for both of them if he stayed away, and let that be the last discussion between them until he marr—

His mind balked and shied away from completing the remainder of that thought.

No good could come in continuing to see Caroline; the woman he yearned for as he'd never yearned for anyone.

And yet, he proved stupid or powerless or mayhap both, for he could not let their latest meeting, be their last. He could not leave her upset.

It was why the moment he'd seen her take flight, he'd set out in pursuit.

It was why even now he made his way into the very gardens she'd raced into. His boots kicked up gravel and small stones as he went and wanting to give Caroline some alert of his arrival, he made no attempt to lighten his steps.

Then he saw her.

Until he drew his last breath, he'd remember her as she was in this moment.

She rested with her back against the wall; a halo of moonlight circling her frame. She was a daughter of the Titans Hyperion and Theia, with temples built to honor her.

"You shouldn't be here," she said softly.

"I know." Were they discovered together; it would be ruinous for the honorable intentions he carried for Lady Beatrice.

Instead, he drifted closer. "Forgive me," he said quietly. "I did not mean to upset you earlier."

She shook her head slightly. "Why are you here?"

This is what she'd say? *What else did you expect? That after the way you parted, she'd be jubilant at seeing you again.* "I wanted to talk with you," he said weakly.

"What could we possibly have to speak about, my lord?"

Nothing. Everything.

Now, however, she'd call him 'my lord'.

He missed her as she used to be with him. He missed them how they used to be together. He wanted to go back to all the other moments where they spoke freely and where she told him her thoughts and he told her his.

Wynn tried again. "I need you to understand."

She stared at him.

She would make him say it. And he was a coward that it was near impossible to get the words out. "About Lady Beatrice." Only, even as he'd spoken aloud the name of the woman he would—needed—to wed, he could not manage a single sentence more. Because something in discussing her with this woman was the height of wrong. Not because Caroline was not someone he didn't trust or respect, but rather, she was a woman he loved.

His heart froze and then thumped slowly, sickeningly

in his chest. He loved her. He loved her spirit and her courage. He loved that she flew kites and thought nothing of playing with her niece and his sister. He loved that she should know everything she did about flowers and—

Caroline gave him a strange long. "Wynn?"

And she could never be his.

Not when his family was in the situation they were in. His eyes slid shut.

Her question cut across the quiet. "Do you love her?"

His eyes flew open. "No."

That admission slipped out entirely too easy.

"And yet, you'd marry her anyway." There was something faintly pleading in her voice, and the sound of it threatened to break him.

"It is different," he implored; needing her to understand, and yet constrained, still. They were getting into dangerous territory. Things he could not and should not talk about. "Most marriages are made for reasons that have nothing to do with love."

Caroline pushed herself from that wall and drifted closer. "That wasn't what I asked," she murmured.

His throat constricted. "I did not realize it was a question."

She stopped before him; still a pace away so that she could effortlessly meet his gaze still, but so very close that the apple blossom scent of her, headier and more fragrant than any and all the flowers in this garden combined flooded his senses. Unbidden he closed his eyes once more and drank in the smell of her.

Caroline eyed him a long while, and then gave her head a sad, pitying look. "You cannot even speak honestly with me."

All the frustration and fear and regret boiled up inside

him. Suddenly, he snapped. He took that last step she'd kept between them, closing that divide. "*All* men have responsibilities," he whispered furiously. "*Some* of us, however, have greater ones; ones we must fulfill; ones that dictate who we wed—"

"And who you don't," she quietly interrupted. "Perfectly respectable women like my sister, Lettie, and now Lady Beatrice?"

And then there was Caroline. Beyond his reach because of the scandal that would forever be attached to her name.

As if she'd heard those unspoken thoughts, her lips quirked in a sad smile that broke his heart all over again. "But certainly not ladies with scandalous pasts." She edged her chin up. "You are no different than anyone else in Polite Society."

He was deserving of her condemnation, and yet it grated, still. "You know nothing of it," he said tightly.

"Because you won't speak of it. What I do know, however, is that you are a hypocrite, my lord."

Heat rushed his cheeks. "I beg your pardon?"

"You'd call me out for my entertaining the idea of marriage to the duke, and yet you'd speak to me about your obligations?" A sound of disgust escaped her. "You men and your insistence on women possessing lily-white reputations, while you carry on with your mistresses and widows and actresses."

It was a double standard, he knew as much. Caroline gave him a harsh once-over, and he was deserving of that icy look. "For all the ways I admired you for being a man who didn't send servants to pick up flowers for the woman he was courting, and for being a devoted brother, and a man who was very good with younger children, you are no different." Clutching her skirts, Caroline snapped them close, and marched around him.

He should let her go.

She'd formed an opinion of him, one that wasn't incorrect; about his intentions and he should allow her to all of it.

Because it didn't matter.

Ultimately, he would be left with the chore of doing the thing he must do to save his family—as much as the Mastersons could be saved.

His marrying a highly respectable lady and having a perfectly respectable marriage would blunt some of the disdain, and it would also ensure that when the scandal hit, he was married and there was a marchioness so there might then be an heir, all of which he wouldn't give ten damns to Sunday about were it not for the fact he'd two younger sisters and a mother whose care he was responsible for.

"Sometimes…a gentlemen must marry." Where he didn't want. "Sometimes, some of us have no choice," he called after her when she continued walking.

This time, she came to a stop.

She turned slowly back around. "You've already said as much." Several paces away, he felt the heat of her stare as she moved it searchingly over his face. "There is always a choice." She spoke with such a gentleness and assurance, he couldn't stop the laugh steeped in cynicism from spilling out.

"Only naïveness or innocence would allow such a response," he said, raking a tired hand through his hair.

Caroline flashed a smile that was both sad and cynical; the latter belying those descriptors he'd assigned her. "I'm certainly not naïve, and I've not been innocent for a long time."

He tensed, as a vitriolic rage, coupled with agony at the hurt she'd known because of another man.

And I am hurting her, too...in a different way. That realization gutted him, and when he spoke, his words came out sharper than she deserved.

"You know nothing of it," he gritted out. "Nor can I speak of it." He dragged a hand through his hair again. It was the closest he'd come to speaking of it with anyone who was not his mother. Not his best friend. Certainly, not his sisters. Something, however, about this particular woman made it so easy for him to talk to and made him want to share.

"No." Fire flashed in Caroline's eyes. "But you know of my scandal and my reasoning and yet question why I should believe that the love I wished for and speak of might somehow come to me."

He flared his nostrils. "You would chastise me for marrying where there is not love, and yet, you yourself speak as though one who has given up on the idea of it for herself."

She tipped her chin at a defiant angle. "Gentlemen don't court me. And the respectable ones,"—*Men like him; her meaning hung clear in the air*—"the ones who do find love, do so with respectable ladies who don't have scandals tied to their names."

"That—"

"Isn't always the case?" Caroline quirked an eyebrow. "The only way for a lady to marry is when a gentleman courts her, and a gentleman does not court a woman with a scandal, and it is disingenuous of you to suggest anything to the contrary, Wynn."

She...wasn't wrong.

In fact, she was very right.

And he hated himself for it.

And more, he hated that he did not have the freedom to let his heart decide what his future should and would be.

For what would his life have been if he'd courted her and not her sister? What would it be were it not for Alice's ruin bearing down on his family? His future would be with her.

No, he could not speak of the reasons he must marry Lady Beatrice. And yet... He briefly closed his eyes. Suddenly, it seemed very important that this woman understand his motives, that Caroline know he wasn't just some pompous bastard obsessed with having a wife who was flawless in every way. "Someone I care deeply about was hurt," he spoke carefully, "in a similar way as you, and...if those—*when* those circumstances are discovered, it will be ruinous to my family."

"One of your sisters," she said softly.

Wynn hesitated a moment, and then he found himself nodding. He'd guarded this from everyone. What was it about this woman that made him feel he could share freely, without fear of voicing aloud those dangerous truths? And then suddenly, the truth came tumbling forth, and he was helpless to stop it. "My family owns an estate in Scotland, and each summer we spend time on those properties," he explained quietly, speaking aloud words he'd never breathed before now. "Unbeknownst to me, a neighboring lord...courted my sister. He flirted with her and..." He paused haltingly, searching for some other way to say it. Only there wasn't. "Whereas society believed you ruined, she in fact, was...*is*." He grimaced. "And soon, society will discover just...how ruined."

Understanding flashed in Caroline's eyes.

She knew.

"Oh, Wynn," she said softly, and unlike before, there was a gentleness to her tone. She seemed to weigh her words a moment. "I know the fear of that, and that in itself is crippling."

A thought slipped in. Of Caroline then, near in age to his sister now, living in dread that the worst thing that could have happened to her after she'd made love with a man who didn't deserve her, might come true—as had happened to his sister.

Wynn balled his fists; wanting to kill that cad as much as he wanted to end the bounder who'd hurt his sister.

Caroline gave her head a wry shake. "There is no greater hypocrisy. Gentlemen can litter London with bastards, freely and without recrimination, and yet if a woman finds herself in a vulnerable situation, then we are shunned, outcasts, ruined for all time."

"Yes, it is hypocrisy at its finest." He released a tired sigh. "And yet, that is the world in which we live."

If the world had been different, he would even now be betrothed to this woman, and not courting another. His chest seized up, spasming in a way that threatened to take him down.

Caroline held his eyes. "Your secret—her secret—I will not share it."

"I know," he said, and he did. He trusted her. "That is why," he whispered, "I cannot freely follow my heart, Caroline." That was why he must marry a lady above reproach. That part he could not speak aloud. To do so would be an insult to this woman before him.

"I know," she murmured, dipping her gaze to his cravat. And this time, there wasn't that biting edge, but rather, a resignation.

He hated himself all the more for he knew she did

see, that she took his words as the unintended—though actual—insult it was.

Caroline made to slip around him, but Wynn caught her lightly by the arm. "Don't go."

Something shifted in the air. It hung heavy between them, more powerful than the most fragrant flower they'd talked and laughed over that day in the London hothouse.

CHAPTER 16

Wynn wanted to kiss her.

Having known his embrace before, Caroline felt it hover in the air.

And more, she wanted it, too.

"We should not be here," she begged, closing her eyes, willing herself to listen to the very words she spoke.

"No." His voice contained the same hoarse desperation as her own.

Settling his hand on her waist, the heat of his touch practically burning Caroline through the fabric of her gown, Wynn lowered his head so that his chin rested against her temple. "I want you, Caroline. In every way. And it is killing me," he whispered harshly into her ear.

How was it possible for her heart to both leap and break at the same time?

His fingers gripped her harder; as he sank them into the fabric of her dress, she felt that firm, desperate hold all the way to her core. Caroline bit her lower lip.

With a shaky sigh, she angled her head and leaned up,

as he leaned in to take her mouth in an angry, almost punishing kiss.

He devoured her, and she devoured him in return.

None of the embraces she'd known in the whole of her life could have prepared her for this.

Wynn consumed her.

As if he sought to imprint the feel and taste of her mouth on his own flesh.

Warmth settled in her belly, and Caroline brought her hands up, curling her fingers in the fabric of his jacket. Dragging herself closer, she pressed shamelessly against him.

Wynn teased his fingers along her jaw, coaxing her to open, and she let her lips part, and he slipped inside.

She touched her tongue to his; tentatively at first, timid little slashes, and yet every stroke of his flesh against hers sent a greater heat through her; and there took on a desperation to her movements.

No dream could have prepared her for this kiss. No romantic book she'd snuck from her sister and denied reading. Nothing.

Wynn filled his palms with her buttocks, scooping her against him, and she moaned; her hips moving rhythmically as she felt the prod of his length against the flat of her belly. Caroline moved against him wantonly, eagerly. Freed by his embrace and the feel of his hands on her.

He set her down on the edge of a nearby bench, and with a knowledge as old as Eve's, Caroline slipped her legs open, and he stepped between them; the noisy rustle of muslin, hedonistic. He edged her dress up, the cooler air kissing her legs, and she whimpered, that soft, desperate sound swallowed by his kiss.

She lifted her hips, arching towards him, needing

something.

And then he gripped her thighs; sinking his fingers into that flesh, and she moaned.

Suddenly, Wynn broke the kiss; his chest heaved madly, in time to her own rapidly moving one. He whispered harshly against her mouth. "We should stop."

"I will never forgive you if you do," she rasped, and gripping him firmly by the neck, she guided his mouth back to hers.

Still, he resisted. "You deserve—"

"We each have our responsibilities, Wynn," she said, her breath coming quickly. "I know that. I don't…expect anything more from you." She knew what her fate was. And worse, she knew what his fate was.

Passion darkened his eyes; those piercing eyes he passed over her.

He was respectable. Honorable. It was why he battled with himself.

"I want you," she breathed against his mouth, pressing her shaking palms against his chest; under her palms she felt the strong, steadying beat of his racing heart—a heart that raced for her. Because of her. It was a powerful aphrodisiac. "If we can't have each other, we can still have this night."

His eyes went a shade darker.

Wynn drew in a noisy, uneven breath. "You don't—"

"Know what I'm saying?" she supplied for him. Caroline angled her head back a fraction to meet his gaze with the same boldness she'd once possessed and had since thought long-dead. But it wasn't. It was alive, and well, and that truth enlivened her. "You're not taking anything I don't want to give." The air crackled like the ground had before the latest lightning strike. "I want this, Wynn.

I want this moment with you." If she was to have a cold, emotionless union, and Wynn was to one day soon marry another, she'd at least have this of him.

Near as they were, with his thick dark lashes, swept low, she could not mistake the heat burning from that gaze locked with hers.

And this time, as she tipped her head back, and he lowered his, there was no more imagining or wondering… it was real.

His lips covered hers a second time, and a little sigh slipped out, and she twined her arms about the nape of his neck, as though it were the most natural thing in the world. Because it was.

Being in his arms felt right, and she wanted this kiss. Not just because when this moment ended, she'd be left with her only prospect of a husband, an ancient, lecherous duke her mother would prove unrelenting in her quest to see Caroline wed. Rather, it was because of the man who held her now.

There was nothing gentle about their kiss; it grew increasingly powerful as he slanted his mouth over hers again and again.

She whimpered, curling her fingers in the overlong silken strands; he swept inside, deepening the kiss, taking her mouth, and she wanted to give it to him. She wanted to give it all to him.

Desire spread a delicious warmth through her; touching every corner, like a flame kindling to life, and then coming to a slow and vibrant awakening.

Wynn slid his hands down her hips like a man memorizing the feel of her, and then he cupped her under her buttocks, drawing her close.

She moaned feeling the long, rigid length of his desire.

And his was a desire…for her.

After the shame and humiliation of Dylan's betrayal, Caroline had been left with the mortified understanding that she'd been courted not because her suitor had yearned for her, but rather he'd wanted the riches that came from marrying her, enough that he'd feigned desire. It had been a blow to her confidence and self-esteem. She'd come to believe she could never inspire passion in any man. But in Wynn's arms, with his hands trembling as he passed them searchingly over her body, she flamed heady with feminine power. With that, the last flimsy chain of restraint snapped free, and she let herself come undone.

Caroline gripped him harder by the nape even as she pressed herself against him, rubbing in a way that felt both natural and forbidden, all at the same time.

He groaned a single word, "Caroline."

That was it.

Nothing more than her name; three syllables she'd heard uttered from countless people for the whole of her life, but something in hearing this man speak it in this way set her ablaze.

She touched her tongue to his over and over. The two of them alternately dancing and dueling, and it was a battle she was all content to lose.

Not breaking contact with her lips, Wynn sank onto the earthen floor, and drew her down atop him; draping her legs around his waist, rucking her skirts up about them in a naughty way.

Anyone might stumble upon them, and she'd be ruined for a second time. And society would be right in everything they said. And she did not care. Not this moment. Not tomorrow. Not thirty years from now, when she was old, and likely the widow of the only man, a decrepit duke, who'd marry her.

The sun and the soft spring breeze alternately kissed her skin along with his touch.

She whimpered as he caught her lower right leg, stroking her calf, squeezing and exploring the limb.

"You are so magnificent," he rasped between kisses.

Caroline whimpered.

She wasn't. But when he spoke in those husky tones, his speech guttural, she could almost believe it.

He lowered the neckline of her dress, and her breath caught, and she stared on as he drew the pebbled tip of her breast into his mouth and suckled.

Caroline's eyes slid shut, and on a moan, she tangled her fingers in his hair, holding him close, guiding him closer. She moved her hips in a way that should shame her into stopping, and yet, she could not muster even a feigned ounce of that sentiment.

The heat of his mouth; the noisy, wet suckling sounds enflamed her.

Wynn cupped her buttocks in his large, powerful palms, and guided her hips, in those wicked undulations.

Caroline's thrusting grew more urgent, as she pushed herself against the hard line of his erection.

Then, Wynn slipped a hand between them, finding her with his fingers.

He consumed her gasp with his mouth; but did not cease that blissful torment he wrought; teasing the nub there, sliding a finger inside her shamefully wet channel and stroking her slowly, expertly.

Caroline whimpered; the force of her hungering too much, and breaking the kiss, she buried her face against his shoulder.

Unrelenting in the pleasure so acute it bordered at pain; Wynn continued that glide of his long finger, adding a second. Caroline's undulations grew frantic.

"Wynn," she moaned, the wool of his jacket muting her voice, muffling it.

And then he stopped.

Caroline cried out; the sound stifled by the fabric of his coat.

But he only set her aside a moment, removed his jacket, and tossed it down as a makeshift bedding.

He paused a moment longer, giving her a look; one that said they could stop. That the decision to continue or not, belonged to her. And for a woman who'd ceased to be seen by the world, beyond anything more than the scandal she'd caused, this control he ceded was powerful stuff.

Sliding to her feet, Caroline held his eyes, and then lowering herself to the ground, she held her arms up.

He was in them in a moment. Their mouths met in an explosive kiss; and there was none of the previous gentleness; only an almost violent tangle of their tongues.

"You deserve more than this," he rasped between kissing her. He pushed her skirts up to her waist, and found her with his fingers, threading them through the patch of curls at her womanhood. "If I were the respectable, honorable man the world takes me for, I'd stop."

"Because you are that man, you let the decision rest with me," she countered. Whimpering, Caroline lifted into his touch. A pressure built at her core; a sharp ache, that only grew more pointed at every glide of his fingers.

He groaned, and then paused to remove that hand, but he was only reaching between them, and freeing his length.

Wynn shifted over her, and she felt the tip of his shaft

prod her entrance. Sweat beaded at his brow; a brow creased as if he were a man in pain, and he slid slowly inside her, stretching Caroline.

Years earlier, Caroline's mother had insisted the moment a man and woman coupled was uncomfortable, distasteful but necessary. When she'd given herself to Dylan, Caroline had learned her mother had been correct. The moment had been painful and awkward but fortunately quick. Even Dylan's kisses had left Caroline unmoved and believing she was incapable of feeling passion.

But she'd been wrong.

And mayhap her mother had merely lied, too. Mayhap all mothers lied, because they knew the moment a woman experienced this wonderment and bliss with one man, there was no turning back from it; that every woman to taste passion like this would only long for more; reputation and the world's opinion, be damned.

As he moved within her; stroking her with his length, Caroline met his downward thrust with an upward one; there was no pain. None at all, in fact.

When last there'd been blood and discomfort; this time there was none.

There was only this glorious, acute pleasure.

Caroline wrapped her arms about Wynn, clinging to him, as she matched her movements to his. There grew a frenzy to their thrusting; and Caroline moaned as that sensation grew somehow sharper; her body climbing higher, so very close to…something she could not name. "Wynn," she pleaded; needing him to relieve that pressure; needing him…wanting him, in every way.

He kissed her. "Caroline," he panted; gripping her hips hard, as if using her to leverage himself.

The muscles of his face grew strained. "Come for me,"

he ordered, a harsh, raspy command of a man who knew precisely what he wanted, and expected, and it was her. And the truth of that sent her over the most magnificent cliff.

Caroline bit her lip to keep from crying out; she arched her back and twisted, as wave after wave sucked her into a glorious heady of bright light and sensation.

Wynn continued to drive within her; ringing every last bit of pleasure from her, as with a gasp, Caroline collapsed into the folds of his shirt.

Wynn gave several more jerks of his hips, and then with a low, guttural groan, befitting a wounded, primal beast, he withdrew from her, and spent himself sideways into the grass.

She stared on fascinated by that shimmery arc of his seed, and then with a sharp gasp of breath, he collapsed atop her; catching himself at the elbows to keep from crushing her.

They lay that way; as their ragged breathing at last grew even; the sounds of the spring; the noisy chirp of the warblers nighttime song, and the bubbling fountain overtook the previous din of her and Wynn's desire, that had drowned out everything else.

Before now.

Now, reality slipped back in.

She stiffened.

Or was that his body?

Mayhap it was the both of them.

Wynn pushed himself from her.

"Caroline," he began, and the touch of regret contained within those three syllables made a liar of her; she'd thought she'd only ever love the sound of her name on his lips. But not like this. Not with regret.

"Do not say anything," she said, her voice emerging sharper than she intended. "I wanted this, and I don't have any regrets."

He brushed a kiss against her temple; that brush of his lips so tender it brought her eyes closed. "What was it?" he murmured.

Dazed, she sought to make sense of what he was asking.

"You spoke once about that wish you made upon the star. What was it?"

Caroline laughed softly. "To always be as happy as I'd been in that moment. It was a silly one; a child's wish." Because a person couldn't really ever be happy always. And as an adult one discovered just how elusive that gift in fact, was.

Something darkened in his eyes, and she thought for a moment he intended to say more.

But he didn't…and reality intruded its ugly head.

They didn't speak another word.

And it was only a short while later, after he'd gently cleaned her, and helped her with her dress and hair, and then parted ways, she admitted that she'd lied to him. And herself.

She did have regrets.

One moment with Wynn would never be enough.

Ever.

CHAPTER 17

Seated in his office, a pen in his fingers, Wynn stared distractedly over the top of them at nothing in particular.

He'd made love to her.

Not only had he made love to her, he'd done so in Lord and Lady Stanhope's gardens...just beyond prying eyes.

There came a light rap at the door.

He glanced up from his miserable musings. Each sister had an identifying manner of knocking at the door. This hesitant one belonging to Alice, and guilt knotted his belly. "Enter," he called to the eldest of his sisters.

Sure enough, the oak panel opened a fraction, and Alice dipped her head around the edge before tentatively entering the room and shutting the door behind her.

"What is it?" he asked, finding his voice, and his feet, he came around the desk to meet her. He'd been old enough to recall the miserable time of it their mother had when she was expecting. There'd been frequent bouts of sickness; frequent weeping. All of it enough to make a chap want to spare any woman that suffering and forego the heir. "Is everything all right?"

Alice lifted sad eyes to his. "No."

Worry filled him. "Should I—"

"That is, I am fine," Alice interrupted. "I'm referring to you, big brother."

Big brother.

It was that affectionate moniker she'd forever attached to him; since she'd been a girl of four, and he more than a decade her senior, and it only reminded him of all the ways he'd not protected her; all the ways he'd failed to keep her safe.

"You do know…it is not your fault?" she asked softly.

Wynn didn't pretend to misunderstand. "It is." If he'd been aware, if he'd paid attention to the fact his sister had been rushing off to meet a man who'd never been worthy of her, she'd not be in the way she was now.

His sister studied him contemplatively. "I've always felt quite badly for other ladies. They've had roguish brothers, who, the moment they went to university forgot about their families; and became so fixated on their own pleasures and pastimes that they never had time to remember them." She flashed a sad smile. "But that was never you. You were never one who bothered much with those ways, and you weren't one who forgot me or Elspeth. You treated us as people who you enjoyed being around. I always admired you for that."

"Because I do enjoy being with you," he said simply. He loved his sisters. It was why he had to protect them at all costs. Protect them, as he'd already failed.

Alice held a palm up. "I've not finished."

"Forgive me," he murmured. "As you were."

"I always admired you." She paused and speared him with a sharper gaze than he'd ever before had turned his way by her. "Until now."

His gut clenched.

"And do you know why I can't admire you?" she asked into the silence; taking a step forward.

Wynn managed to shake his head. "I suspect it is because—"

"It is because you would sacrifice yourself and your happiness for me. Do you truly believe wedding where your heart doesn't lead will somehow help me? That it will somehow undo my mistake, and restore my virtue, and make any of this go away?'

He stared dumbly at her.

Alice took another step. "Because it won't, Wynn. None of this can be undone, and certainly not by you giving up on a woman whom you truly love because her reputation is deemed black by society's standards."

Hearing his rejection of Caroline painted that way, caused a sharp ache in his chest.

"I cannot marry Beatrice," he whispered.

His sister smiled the first smile in longer than Wynn could remember. "It took you long enough."

Yes, it had. Though, he suspected he'd known that all along.

Nay, not all along.

Just as he knew he *wanted* to marry Caroline. Needed to. Needed, not because of any sense of obligation—though honor did dictate he do right by her. Rather, it was a need that came from the love he carried for her. The need to spend every day making her happy and laugh; and not going to flower shops in the hopes of seeing her, but actually going with her and learning every last detail she had to impart about the blooms in that place, and every place, because he could listen to her every day. And he wanted to.

And it surely spoke to his failings as a brother that he wanted this, his happiness with her, above all else… despite their reputations and the scandal bearing down on them.

His sister laid a gentle hand on his sleeve. "It does not mean you are a terrible brother. It means you are the best of ones for showing that love matters most. That, regardless of how society has deemed a woman unworthy, you see that she is…" Tears glittered in his sister's eyes. "And it gives me hope…"

That someday, some man fight feel the same way for her.

Only, there couldn't be. There was no man, regardless of whatever scandal surrounded Alice, who could ever be deserving of her.

And for the first time, in longer than he could remember, Wynn felt…free.

"Thank you," he said hoarsely.

Her smile widening, Alice went up on tiptoe and kissed his cheek. "Do not thank me. Thank *you* for not making me feel miserable for the rest of my days about the fact that you are miserable the rest of your days because of something I did."

Emotion filled his chest. How selfless she was. She deserved so much better, and so much more.

"Mother is going to be disappointed," he gently warned; needing to prepare her for that truth.

"Mother is already disappointed."

He and Alice whipped their focus to the front of the room to where their mother stood with her arms folded at her chest. Pushing the door shut, she started forward.

Oh, hell. "Moth—"

"Not a word," she said, with a wave of her hand. "You are not marrying Lady Beatrice, then."

There was a long moment of silence before Wynn managed to find his voice, and then he did. "I'm not. Because I don't love her. I'm—"

"—in love with Lady Caroline," she finished for him. She gave him a once over, and then shorted. "Took you long enough."

Wynn froze? Took him long enough?

Her eyes twinkled. "What I was going to say is I'm already disappointed that it took you so long to realize your heart matters, too, Wynn." Her gaze grew solemn. "I love you and want you to be happy."

Relief suffused every part of his chest. "I love you, too, Mother."

Watching the exchange between mother and son, Alice dabbed at her tear-filled eyes. "I quite despise this, you know. I'm given to waterworks at the least provocation."

He fished out his kerchief and handed it over.

Accepting the scrap of white fabric, his sister blew noisily.

Knock-knock-knock-knock-knock. Knock–

"Knock," he called out the expected response to that familiar greeting used only by his youngest sister.

He and Alice looked to the front of the room. "Hey… popp…" His greeting faded, as Elspeth entered alongside her friend.

A familiar friend, one that reminded him of another.

Kicking the door shut closed with the heel of her boot, Elspeth didn't so much as greet their sister. "I've brought someone, Wynn."

"I see that," he said, bending low at the waist, as Alice and Violet exchanged greetings.

Violet turned to Wynn. "You don't have to bow. I'm here on business," Caroline's niece explained, with deadly serious eyes.

"That sounds important," he said with a suitable modicum of somberness.

"It is," Elspeth confirmed. "Very." His youngest sister folded her arms. "Caroline is getting married."

Yes, she was. Should it come as any surprise that his sister had gathered his intentions.

Somewhere between here and Hyde Park, he'd known what he would do.

He'd known he would marry her. A smile formed on his lips. He'd known—

"To a duke," Violet supplied.

Wynn froze.

The problem was someone else had realized it, too.

Nay, not someone else. Wynn's heart thumped at a slow, sickening thud against the walls of his chest. "What?" he whispered.

"Grandmere is adamant she marry the Duke of Lennox."

A curse exploded from Alice's lips. "That old lech?"

That old lech who'd been ogling her at the ball.

She wouldn't.

She couldn't.

Only, she'd alluded to the fact that she would.

"I believe she will," Violet said matter-of-factly, confirming at some point he'd spoken aloud, and yet everything was all twisted in his mind; jumbled and distorted; like he was swimming, upside down, under water. "You might not know it, but Grandmere is rather terrible, and has a way of making Aunt Caroline feel *very* bad about herself."

"That is just terrible," Wynn's mother murmured.

It was terrible for Caroline.

And she'd escape.

She'd see there were no other prospects; or hopes for a good, honorable gentleman, because no good, honorable gentleman had given her reason to believe she was worthy of those things—when she was in fact, everything. Every man had made her feel somehow less for the fact she'd been deceived and left with the tattered remnants of a reputation that society would never let be put back together.

Me. I made her feel that way, too.

Wynn's eyes slid shut of their own volition, as self-loathing held him in its grip.

And for it, Caroline would marry that vile letch.

"Wynn?"

Once engaged, Caroline would be gone to him.

"*Wynn?*"

And where he'd found himself the same way, two times prior; being too late, as different men had stepped forward and up to wed women Wynn had been courting, this time it was different.

"Wynn?" his mother clapped her hands sharply before his eyes; bringing him back to this hellish present.

"Is something wrong with your brother?" Violet was asking Wynn's sister.

No. Everything was wrong.

This time I'll not survive.

"I have to go," he barked; already bolting for the door.

"*We* have to go," Elspeth said, and perhaps if there'd been more time, perhaps if every moment passed, wasn't a moment lost, he'd have objected.

But a short while later, after one quick stop, Wynn

found himself jumping from his horse before a familiar household and tossing the reins to a waiting servant.

It wasn't the first such walk he'd made to this very household, with these same intentions.

Though, in fairness, this wasn't a walk.

It was more of a run.

The kind of run that earned him stares from passersby, and the kind that would have at one time horrified him enough into slowing down.

Wynn took the steps two at a time and pounded hard on the door.

A door that was opened so quickly, he nearly pummeled the poor servant standing on the other side of it.

"My—"

Pushing his way past the startled butler, he paused briefly as he caught sight of the three ladies already gathered in the foyer.

His sisters and Violet glared at him.

"It took you long enough," Violet muttered.

"Too long," his youngest sister added.

Too long.

Wynn's heart dropped. He was too late. That stop had felt important, and yet, it hadn't been as important as getting here before the duke and—

He stilled.

And it *wasn't* too late.

As long as she wasn't married, and Wynn wasn't, then it wasn't too late.

There'd be a scandal if she broke a betrothal, but what was a little scandal compared to love.

Wynn took off running, bellowing one name: "*Caroline!*"

CHAPTER 18

After Lord Somerville's betrayal, Caroline had resolved to never again be scandalous.

She'd sworn she would never do anything to merit her mother's shame, or society's.

She would do everything that was expected of her.

And she'd done an admirable job of it.

Until this day. The day she'd informed her mother that she would reject the Duke of Lennox's offer of marriage.

"You are mad," her mother barked; pacing back and forth before the white upholstered sofa, whose edge, Caroline sat stiffly upon; her palms folded on her lap. "Utterly mad. What are you *thinking*?"

"I am thinking I do not love him."

"*Love*!" Her mother stopped abruptly and towered over Caroline. "You would speak about love? Did you not learn firsthand the effects of love?"

That charge would have once hurt. No longer.

"Miles and Phillipa are in love and happy as are Lettie and Anthony, and Rhys and—"

Her mother cut her off. "There is one difference between you and them. Those ladies were not ruined as you were, Caroline." She gave her head a slight shake. "Now," she said, her voice measured once more, "do stop being impractical and come meet His Grace."

"What is the meaning of this?"

They looked over as Miles entered the parlor. As if it were the most natural thing in the world, he'd perched high on his shoulders his young son, the boy he and Philippa had adopted four years earlier.

Relief filled her.

Paddie waved his hand excitedly. "Hullo, Auntie Caroline. Is Grandmother yelling at you?"

She returned the wave and nodded. "I fear she is."

Caroline's mother turned to Miles. "Thank goodness you are here. Your sister is being unreasonable. Perhaps you can talk sense into her," she said, without so much as a greeting for Miles and Philippa's cherished son whom she had never treated as a grandson.

Though, in fairness, Caroline's mother treated all her children and grandchildren in that disinterested way.

"And just what sense am I talking into Caroline?"

"The Duke of Lennox has come to offer her marriage and she is being difficult."

Her brother and mother both looked at Caroline.

"Is this true, Caroline?" Miles asked.

"That the duke is here to offer or I'm being difficult?"

Miles's lips twitched. "Either?"

Caroline nodded. "Both."

The dowager threw her hands up. "And she's making light." Their mother stormed over, and all but slapped the newspaper against his chest. "The front pages, Miles. They are *still* writing about your sister and—" As if she'd finally remembered her young grandson was present, she glanced down. "And you know..."

Caroline curled her toes sharply as she was transported back to a different time; to the worst time when she'd been forced to speak with Miles about her ruin. Odd that this didn't feel any easier.

Unable to meet his gaze, she looked away as he set Paddie down.

A groan escaped her.

Paddie gave her fingers another tug. "Aunt Caro, are you all right? You sound like how I sound when I'm going to be sick. Do you need a chamber pot?"

She actually rather thought she might. Caroline forced a smile for the child's benefit. "I am fine, sweet. Just fine."

"Paddie, why do you not run along and find your mother in the breakfast room before she leaves for the day."

The little boy's eyes lightened, even as his grandmother's face tightened at the reminder of Philippa's work at the school she'd begun here in London to provide education to children who struggled to hear and see and others who were subject to the unkindness of the world at large.

Paddie paused only long enough to offer Caroline another—this time—hasty hug, before bolting off and leaving the adults alone.

For a long moment, her gaze followed his flight with no little amount of envy coursing through her.

Caroline wanted to run.

But running was only second to falling in the list of horrifying things a lady must never do.

The moment Paddie had gone, the dowager launched into Caroline. "It is bad enough that you let yourself be so ruined by that...that Scottish fortune hunter," she seethed. "But now, you will reject a *duke*?"

"As she should!" Miles snapped. "What woman would truly, ever wish to wed one such as *Lennox*?"

"A desperate one," the dowager cried out. "A woman with absolutely no prospects, Miles. One with no hope of any future. Not a future that is respectable and—"

"And I'd rather she remain unmarried for the rest of her days than suffer through a marriage to one such as the duke," Miles thundered. That unlikeliest of outbursts from her always-in-control, always-affable brother briefly shook their mother.

Caroline swung her attention between feuding mother and son.

The dowager, however, was never one who'd be rattled for long. "You are being disingenuous, pretending as though having your poor relation sister, too sullied to find a husband, underfoot for the rest of your marriage is something you actually want."

Rage tightened Miles's face. "How dare you?" he seethed. "I have never, *ever* viewed my sisters as a burden." He jabbed a finger her way and wagged it in a circle. "*You*, on the other hand, have been *only* that."

Their mother paled. "You do not know what you are—"

"I know *precisely* what I'm saying," he bellowed. "I want you gone. I want you at any country estate, any property, as long as it isn't this one. I should have done this the moment you rejected my marriage to Philippa."

"Bah, Philippa...who is always off running that silly school—"

"It is an institution that provides hope and futures for young ladies, and now boys, who've not had the benefit of supportive family or resources," Caroline added her support to her generous-in-every-way sister-in-law.

Miles thinned his eyes into dark slits. This time when he

spoke, he did so with a calm and quiet that was somehow more powerful than his earlier shouting. "I've tolerated far too much of how you treated Lettie and Caroline. I will, however, be damned if you harangue Caroline anymore, and then turn your sights on my daughters."

Silence fell.

The dowager stood there stiffly, she gave a slight flounce of her head. "Very well. I see that I'm no longer needed. I shall have my things readied and leave at first light." With her head held high as only a queen might manage, the duchess marched from the room; closing the door behind her with a quiet, in-control click.

The moment Caroline and Miles were alone, she spoke. "Bravo, brother."

He flashed a wan smile. "I'm not deserving of that. It was long overdue." His smile faded, and he came over to join her, falling to a knee alongside her seat. "I am so sorry I've not done more to protect you. First, from Somerville, and then...the fallout with Mother and society."

"Oh, Miles," she said softly. "I'm not a young girl to be protected. I'm a grown woman who made my own decisions." And she was finally at peace with her past. She'd made a mistake, but she didn't need to punish herself forever.

"That does not mean I should not have defended you as you deserved," he whispered, dropping his head.

"You have given me a home and only ever made me feel wanted. And I am grateful," she said.

She had the assurance of her brother that she'd never be a burden. Her mother was gone. This should be enough. And yet...she wanted more.

Caroline caught her lower lip between her teeth, and headed for the door, desperately needing to be alone.

"Caroline?"

She stared at the door panel. Just a pace away. Four feet. So close.

Caroline turned back.

Miles scrubbed a hand down his face. "You're in love." He spoke with all the resignation an older brother could about such a realization.

"Had I not been, I suspect it would have been easier to simply say 'yes' to His Grace." She brushed away an errant tear, but it was only replaced by another. "And knowing he will not marry me, that he cannot marry me, should have made it even easier; but it did not."

"As much as I'd like to trounce the fellow too stupid to know the worth of a woman whose love he's throwing over, I'm grateful to him for being a reason you'd not settle for less than you deserve…with the duke or anyone."

Caroline pressed her eyes shut. Only… "He is not stupid. He is a good man, and a devoted brother who is doing what is best for his family."

Miles came over and took her hand, giving it a gentle squeeze. "I'd only have you marry a man who would do what was best for *you*, first. And someday there will be."

Now he spoke with the absolution only a brother—and one who'd been fortunate enough to find that gift with his wife—could.

Only, there wouldn't be those things he spoke of. Because there was only—

"Caroline!"

She and her brother whipped their gazes to the front of the room just as the door exploded open. The unexpectedness of it sent her stumbling back. Wynn burst into the room, catching her just as her back would have touched the floor.

Heart pounding for so many reasons, Caroline reflexively twined her hands around his nape.

"Wynn?" she whispered. Her thoughts whirred, and she tried to process his being here and what it meant, and yet, all she could utter were three words: "You…caught me."

He blinked slowly. "I did." Then, he gave his head a shake; and as he set her on her feet, a crazed look entered his eyes. "Don't!" he rasped, gasping for breath like one who'd run a great race and then been forced to swim the channel in immediate succession. "Do not wed him!" Wynn's forceful statement ended on the slight, uptilt of a question.

Caroline opened her mouth to speak, just as an audience converged upon them: four young ladies—two of Wynn's sisters—and Caroline's nieces came streaming into the room with a bevy of footmen and the butler at their heels.

Wynn turned his palms up. "I don't know if I'm too late. I've always had shite timing, Caroline."

His sisters cleared their throats.

"Rubbish timing," he automatically corrected.

"I prefer shite," Faith whispered. "He's speaking from the heart."

Miles slapped a hand over his eyes.

"That's why shite shouldn't be a word of choice," Alice returned in an equally noisy whisper.

Caroline beseeched Wynn with her eyes. "Yes?" she whispered, needing him to finish.

"What I'm saying…" Wynn cleared his throat. "What I'm trying to say is…I attempted to marry two women before you."

"That is certainly not what you should say, dear brother," Wynn's eldest sister muttered under her breath.

Caroline's lips twitched.

Wynn ignored that admonishment and took a step closer. "I intended to offer marriage twice before."

"I'm agreeing with our sister on this," Elspeth said. "That part is not needed."

"At least, not twice," Violet volunteered.

"And both of those women rejected me for another." Wynn moved his gaze over her face. "Neither of those times shattered my heart. Both of those times I was unaffected, but if you do this, Caroline, if you marry the duke, or not the duke, even if you marry *any* other man, a man who isn't me, I will be ruined. Wrecked for all time. Because I love you," he said hoarsely, ringing a gasp from Caroline's lips, one she caught belatedly behind trembling fingers. "I love you so desperately and I've been such a bloody arse."

She dimly registered her brother standing and stepping aside, joining Violet and Wynn's sisters several paces away.

The slight Adam's apple in Wynn's throat moved. He lifted the bouquet in his hand. "I should have come straightaway, Caroline."

"Damned straight you should have," Elspeth muttered.

"But you deserved flowers, and then I couldn't just bring any flowers because, well, a clever woman with an impressive bit of knowledge on them taught me that a fellow in love shouldn't just show up with *any* flowers." He stretched those blooms towards her. Several buds missing a petal or two. Others slightly crushed. Never before, however, in all the arrangements she'd seen for her family, or bouquets to her sisters, compared to these. "The daffodil," he pointed to the flower. "Because I hold you in the highest of regards. Because my love for you, Caroline… it is unequalled." Another tear fell. "Chrysanthemum, because I love you most ardently. The camellia because I long for you." Sighs went up from the women who made up their audience. "Myrtle," he finally settled on, "for it represents love in a marriage, and I want that with you. Marriage, and there will be love in it."

Caroline's heart danced, and it was like a thousand butterflies had been set free within her breast. She tried to speak, but Wynn continued on a rush. "Of course, I…also included the geranium," he pointed to the fuchsia flower, "because I've been such a fool, Caroline." He let his arm fall. "Such a bloody fool. How could it take me so very long to see you?" He dropped to a knee, taking the spot where her brother had previously knelt. "But I see you now, and I'm asking—hoping—you see a future with me in it. I—"

Caroline leaned in, kissing the rest of that vow from his lips. "I love you," she whispered against his mouth, and he returned that most tender of embraces.

When he drew back, a dazed grin graced his lips. "Is that a yes?"

"It is."

"Now, given my record, I'd be wise for me to get you to the altar as quick as I'm able."

"Of course." She touched her brow to his. "But only because I do not want to wait any longer to be your wife. After all, you do know what they say?"

"What is that, my heart?"

"Third time is a charm."

And with their families' jubilant laughter and clapping echoing around them, Caroline and Wynn kissed once more.

THE END

Don't miss Defying the Duke, featuring Caroline's sister, Lady Lettie Brookfield!

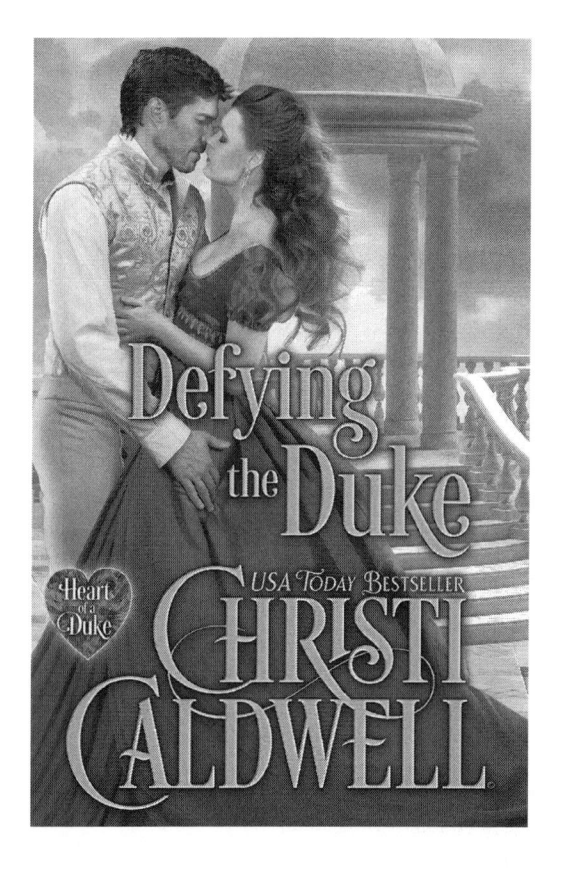

Bookish and spirited, Lady Lettie Brookfield is firmly on the shelf. The last thing she wants, however, is to spend the rest of her days as an unmarried sister, dependent upon her family's charity. Accepting she won't have a love match, she finds herself coming around to the idea of marrying the only suitor she's ever had…that is until she's suddenly reunited with her brother's former best friend, the brooding, formally charming, Anthony, Duke of Granville.

Years earlier, in an unselfish act intended to save his friend, Anthony committed an unforgivable betrayal; one that severed his friendship. Now he's a duke and must fulfill his obligations. The last woman he has any right to long for is his former best friend's younger sister, Lettie.

All grown-up Lettie is passionate, quick-witted, and desirable, and it isn't long before Anthony falls for her, the very last woman he should consider marrying. Will past betrayals keep them apart? Or is there a path to a new beginning with Anthony and the only woman he truly loves?

And be sure and check out the latest installments coming from Christi Caldwell's bestselling Heart of a Duke series!

The Devil and the Debutante

Featuring Lady Faith Brookfield and Rex Dumond, the gaming hell proprietor of Forbidden Pleasures, theirs is a tale of deception, lies, and passion.

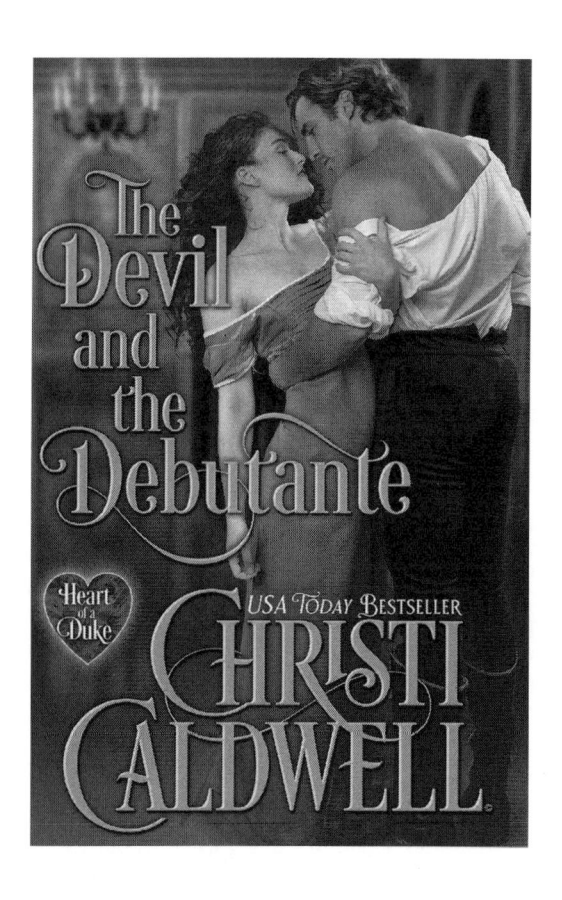

Devil by Daylight

*Featuring Miss Honoria Fairfax and
Tormund Stone, the Earl of Rockford.*

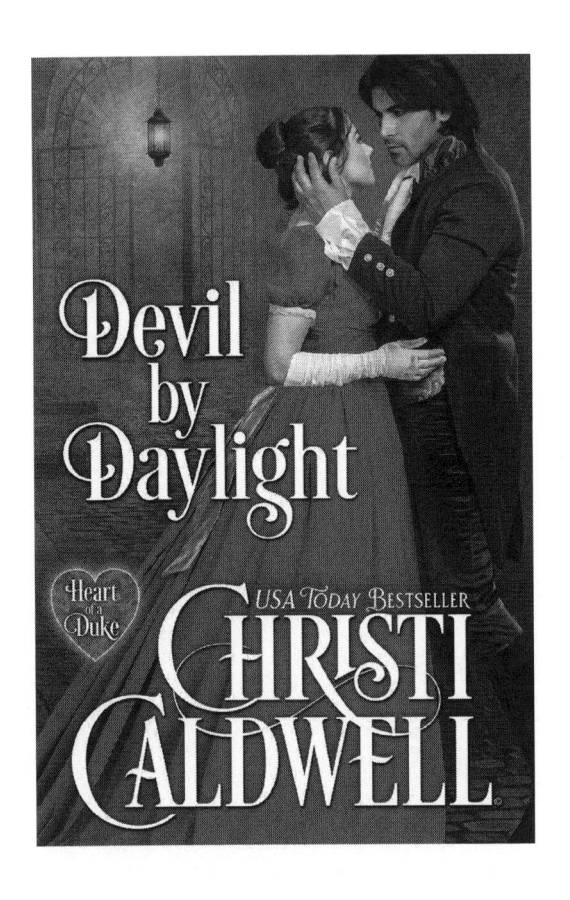

*Also Coming by Christi Caldwell
an Amazon Exclusive*

The Duke Alone

*For an abandoned lady and a reclusive duke, the winter
season brings a swirl of romance—
and danger—in a bracing novel by
USA Today bestselling author Christi Caldwell.*

Lady Myrtle McQuoid has always felt a little forgotten, and this season is no exception. When her boisterous family vacates their London townhouse for the country, Myrtle finds she's been left behind. But she just needs to stay warm, keep her belly full, and distract herself until her relatives realize their mistake and turn back to collect her. Surely that won't take long.

Brooding widower Val Bancroft, the Duke of Aragon, has shut himself off from the world. He craves blessed solitude—a loyal dog, a silent house, and his own company are all he requires. Certainly not the nonstop chattering of the joyful, opinionated young woman next door.

But with a potential threat lurking in the winter shadows, Myrtle may need to pluck up the nerve to approach the reclusive duke. And Val is not one to turn his back on a vulnerable lady.

Amid the silent nights of London, beneath a blanket of snow, could the light of a new, warm love be kindling?

OTHER BOOKS IN THE HEART OF A DUKE SERIES
BY CHRISTI CALDWELL

TO CATCH A VISCOUNT
Book 17 in the "Heart of a Duke" Series

Miss Marcia Gray's cameo-perfect life is destroyed when scandal leaves her standing alone at the altar on her wedding day. Her heart shattered, she decides to embrace her ruined reputation and explore every forbidden pleasure. All she needs is a little help from her long-time friend—and society's most wicked rogue—Andrew Barrett, Viscount Waters.

Andrew tried his hand at love and lost badly, and has no interest in marriage or respectability. Nonetheless, even he knows he should avoid Marcia and her harebrained attempts to embark on a life of impropriety. Andrew, however, has never done what he's supposed to do, nor can he stand about twirling his sword cane while Marcia dabbles in forbidden pleasures without him.

When they push the boundaries too far, Marcia and Andrew must determine whether old secrets will keep them apart, or newfound love can forge a path back to a respectable, shared future.

To Hold a Lady's Secret
Book 16 in the "Heart of a Duke" Series

Lady Gillian Farendale is in trouble. Her titled father has dragged her through one London Season after another, until the sheer monotony of the marriage mart and the last vestige of Gillian's once-independent spirit conspire to lead her into a single night of folly. When her adventure goes so very wrong, she has only one old friend to whom she can turn for help.

Colin Lockhart's youthful friendship with Lady Gillian cost him everything, and a duke's by-blow had little enough to start with. He's survived years on London's roughest streets to become a highly successful Bow Street Runner, and his dream of his own inquiry agency is almost within his grasp.

Then Gillian begs him to once again risk angering her powerful father. The ruthless logic of the street tells Colin that he dare not help Gillian, while his tender heart tempts him to once again risk everything for the only woman he'll ever love.

To Tempt a Scoundrel
Book 15 in the "Heart of a Duke" Series

Never trust a gentleman...

Once before, Lady Alice Winterbourne trusted her heart to an honorable, respectable man... only to be jilted in the scandal of the Season. Longing for an escape from all the whispers and humiliation, Alice eagerly accepts an invitation to her friend's house party. In the country, she hopes to find some peace from the embarrassment left in London... Unfortunately, she finds her former betrothed and his new bride in attendance.

Never love a lady...

Lord Rhys Brookfield has no interest in marriage. Ever. He's worked quite hard at building both his fortune and his reputation as a rogue—and intends to enjoy all that they can offer him. That is if his match-making mother will stop pairing him with prospective brides. When Rhys and Alice meet, sparks flare. But with every new encounter, their first impressions of one another are challenged and an unlikely friendship is forged.

Desperate, Rhys proposes a pretend courtship, one meant to spite Alice's former betrothed and prevent any matchmaking attempts toward Rhys. What neither expects is that a pretense can become so much more. Or that a burning passion can heal... and hurt.

BEGUILED BY A BARON
Book 14 in the "Heart of a Duke" Series

A Lady with a Secret... Partially deaf, with a birthmark marring her face, Bridget Hamilton is content with her life, even if she's been cast out of her family. But her peaceful existence—expanding her mind with her study of rare books—is threatened with an ultimatum from her evil brother—steal a valuable book or give up her son. Bridget has no choice; her son is her world.

A Lord with a Purpose... Vail Basingstoke, Baron Chilton is known throughout London as the Bastard Baron. After battling at Waterloo, he establishes himself as the foremost dealer in rare books and builds a fortune, determined to never be like the self-serving duke who sired him. He devotes his life to growing his fortune to care for his illegitimate siblings, also fathered by the duke. The chance to sell a highly coveted book for a financial windfall is his only thought.

Two Paths Collide... When Bridget masquerades as the baron's newest housekeeper, he's hopelessly intrigued by her quick wit and her skill with antique tomes. Wary from having his heart broken in the past, it should be easy enough to keep Bridget at arm's length, yet desire for her dogs his steps. As they spend time in each other's company, understanding for life grows as does love, but when Bridget's integrity is called into question, Vail's world is shattered—as is his heart again. Now Bridget and Vail will have to overcome the horrendous secrets and lies between them to grasp a love—and life—together.

To Enchant a Wicked Duke
Book 13 in the "Heart of a Duke" Series

A Devil in Disguise

Years ago, when Nick Tallings, the recent Duke of Huntly, watched his family destroyed at the hands of a merciless nobleman, he vowed revenge. But his efforts had been futile, as his enemy, Lord Rutland is without weakness.

Until now…

With his rival finally happily married, Nick is able to set his ruthless scheme into motion. His plot hinges upon Lord Rutland's innocent, empty-headed sister-in-law, Justina Barrett. Nick will ruin her, marry her, and then leave her brokenhearted.

A Lady Dreaming of Love

From the moment Justina Barrett makes her Come Out, she is labeled a Diamond. Even with her ruthless father determined to sell her off to the highest bidder, Justina never gives up on her hope for a good, honorable gentleman who values her wit more than her looks.

A Not-So-Chance Meeting

Nick's ploy to ensnare Justina falls neatly into place in the streets of London. With each carefully orchestrated encounter, he slips further and further inside the lady's heart, never anticipating that Justina, with her quick wit and strength, will break down his own defenses. As Nick's plans begins to unravel, he's left to determine which is more important—Justina's love or his vow for vengeance. But can Justina ever forgive the duke who deceived her?

One Winter with a Baron
Book 12 in the "Heart of a Duke" Series

A clever spinster:

Content with her spinster lifestyle, Miss Sybil Cunning wants to prove that a future as an unmarried woman is the only life for her. As a bluestocking who values hard, empirical data, Sybil needs help with her research. Nolan Pratt, Baron Webb, one of society's most scandalous rakes, is the perfect gentleman to help her. After all, he inspires fear in proper mothers and desire within their daughters.

A notorious rake:

Society may be aware of Nolan Pratt, Baron's Webb's wicked ways, but what he has carefully hidden is his miserable handling of his family's finances. When Sybil presents him the opportunity to earn much-needed funds, he can't refuse.

A winter to remember:

However, what begins as a business arrangement becomes something more and with every meeting, Sybil slips inside his heart. Can this clever woman look beneath the veneer of a coldhearted rake to see the man Nolan truly is?

TO REDEEM A RAKE
Book 11 in the "Heart of a Duke" Series

He's spent years scandalizing society.
Now, this rake must change his ways.

Society's most infamous scoundrel, Daniel Winterbourne, the Earl of Montfort, has been promised a small fortune if he can relinquish his wayward, carousing lifestyle. And behaving means he must also help find a respectable companion for his youngest sister—someone who will guide her and whom she can emulate. However, Daniel knows no such woman. But when he encounters a childhood friend, Daniel believes she may just be the answer to all of his problems.

Having been secretly humiliated by an unscrupulous blackguard years earlier, Miss Daphne Smith dreams of finding work at Ladies of Hope, an institution that provides an education for disabled women. With her sordid past and a disfigured leg, few opportunities arise for a woman such as she. Knowing Daniel's history, she wishes to avoid him, but working for his sister is exactly the stepping stone she needs.

Their attraction intensifies as Daniel and Daphne grow closer, preparing his sister for the London Season. But Daniel must resist his desire for a woman tarnished by scandal while Daphne is reminded of the boy she once knew. Can society's most notorious rake redeem his reputation and become the man Daphne deserves?

To Woo a Widow
Book 10 in the "Heart of a Duke" Series

They see a brokenhearted widow.
She's far from shattered.

Lady Philippa Winston is never marrying again. After her late husband's cruelty that she kept so well hidden, she has no desire to search for love.

Years ago, Miles Brookfield, the Marquess of Guilford, made a frivolous vow he never thought would come to fruition—he promised to marry his mother's goddaughter if he was unwed by the age of thirty. Now, to his dismay, he's faced with honoring that pledge. But when he encounters the beautiful and intriguing Lady Philippa, Miles knows his true path in life. It's up to him to break down every belief Philippa carries about gentlemen, proving that not only is love real, but that he is the man deserving of her sheltered heart.

Will Philippa let down her guard and allow Miles to woo a widow in desperate need of his love?

The Lure of a Rake
Book 9 in the "Heart of a Duke" Series

A Lady Dreaming of Love

Lady Genevieve Farendale has a scandalous past. Jilted at the altar years earlier and exiled by her family, she's now returned to London to prove she can be a proper lady. Even though she's not given up on the hope of marrying for love, she's wary of trusting again. Then she meets Cedric Falcot, the Marquess of St. Albans whose seductive ways set her heart aflutter. But with her sordid history, Genevieve knows a rake can also easily destroy her.

An Unlikely Pairing

What begins as a chance encounter between Cedric and Genevieve becomes something more. As they continue to meet, passions stir. But with Genevieve's hope for true love, she fears Cedric will be unable to give up his wayward lifestyle. After all, Cedric has spent years protecting his heart, and keeping everyone out. Slowly, she chips away at all the walls he's built, but when he falters, Genevieve can't offer him redemption. Now, it's up to Cedric to prove to Genevieve that the love of a man is far more powerful than the lure of a rake.

To Trust a Rogue
Book 8 in the "Heart of a Duke" Series

A rogue

Marcus, the Viscount Wessex has carefully crafted the image of rogue and charmer for Polite Society. Under that façade, however, dwells a man whose dreams were shattered almost eight years earlier by a young lady who captured his heart, pledged her love, and then left him, with nothing more than a curt note.

A widow

Eight years earlier, faced with no other choice, Mrs. Eleanor Collins, fled London and the only man she ever loved, Marcus, Viscount Wessex. She has now returned to serve as a companion for her elderly aunt with a daughter in tow. Even though they're next door neighbors, there is little reason for her to move in the same circles as Marcus, just in case, she vows to avoid him, for he reminds her of all she lost when she left.

Reunited

As their paths continue to cross, Marcus finds his desire for Eleanor just as strong, but he learned long ago she's not to be trusted. He will offer her a place in his bed, but not anything more. Only, Eleanor has no interest in this new, roguish man. The more time they spend together, the protective wall they've constructed to keep the other out, begin to break. With all the betrayals and secrets between them, Marcus has to open his heart again. And Eleanor must decide if it's ever safe to trust a rogue.

To Wed His Christmas Lady
Book 7 in the "Heart of a Duke" Series

She's longing to be loved:

Lady Cara Falcot has only served one purpose to her loathsome father—to increase his power through a marriage to the future Duke of Billingsley. As such, she's built protective walls about her heart, and presents an icy facade to the world around her. Journeying home from her finishing school for the Christmas holidays, Cara's carriage is stranded during a winter storm. She's forced to tarry at a ramshackle inn, where she immediately antagonizes another patron—William.

He's avoiding his duty in favor of one last adventure:

William Hargrove, the Marquess of Grafton has wanted only one thing in life—to avoid the future match his parents would have him make to a cold, duke's daughter. He's returning home from a blissful eight years of traveling the world to see to his responsibilities. But when a winter storm interrupts his trip and lands him at a falling-down inn, he's forced to share company with a commanding Lady Cara who initially reminds him exactly of the woman he so desperately wants to avoid.

A Christmas snowstorm ushers in the spirit of the season:

At the holiday time, these two people who despise each other due to first perceptions are offered renewed beginnings and fresh starts. As this gruff stranger breaks down the walls she's built about herself, Cara has to determine whether she can truly open her heart to trusting that any man is capable of good and that she herself is capable of love. And William has to set aside all previous thoughts he's carried of the polished ladies like Cara, to be the man to show her that love.

The Heart of a Scoundrel
Book 6 in the "Heart of a Duke" Series

Ruthless, wicked, and dark, the Marquess of Rutland rouses terror in the breast of ladies and nobleman alike. All Edmund wants in life is power. After he was publically humiliated by his one love Lady Margaret, he vowed vengeance, using Margaret's niece, as his pawn. Except, he's thwarted by another, more enticing target—Miss Phoebe Barrett.

Miss Phoebe Barrett knows precisely the shame she's been born to. Because her father is a shocking letch she's learned to form her own opinions on a person's worth. After a chance meeting with the Marquess of Rutland, she is captivated by the mysterious man. He, too, is a victim of society's scorn, but the more encounters she has with Edmund, the more she knows there is powerful depth and emotion to the jaded marquess.

The lady wreaks havoc on Edmund's plans for revenge and he finds he wants Phoebe, at all costs. As she's drawn into the darkness of his world, Phoebe risks being destroyed by Edmund's ruthlessness. And Phoebe who desires love at all costs, has to determine if she can ever truly trust the heart of a scoundrel.

To Love a Lord
Book 5 in the "Heart of a Duke" Series

All she wants is security:

The last place finishing school instructor Mrs. Jane Munroe belongs, is in polite Society. Vowing to never wed, she's been scuttled around from post to post. Now she finds herself in the Marquess of Waverly's household. She's never met a nobleman she liked, and when she meets the pompous, arrogant marquess, she remembers why. But soon, she discovers Gabriel is unlike any gentleman she's ever known.

All he wants is a companion for his sister:

What Gabriel finds himself with instead, is a fiery spirited, bespectacled woman who entices him at every corner and challenges his age-old vow to never trust his heart to a woman. But…there is something suspicious about his sister's companion. And he is determined to find out just what it is.

All they need is each other:

As Gabriel and Jane confront the truth of their feelings, the lies and secrets between them begin to unravel. And Jane is left to decide whether or not it is ever truly safe to love a lord.

Loved By a Duke
Book 4 in the "Heart of a Duke" Series

For ten years, Lady Daisy Meadows has been in love with Auric, the Duke of Crawford. Ever since his gallant rescue years earlier, Daisy knew she was destined to be his Duchess. Unfortunately, Auric sees her as his best friend's sister and nothing more. But perhaps, if she can manage to find the fabled heart of a duke pendant, she will win over the heart of her duke.

Auric, the Duke of Crawford enjoys Daisy's company. The last thing he is interested in however, is pursuing a romance with a woman he's known since she was in leading strings. This season, Daisy is turning up in the oddest places and he cannot help but notice that she is no longer a girl. But Auric wouldn't do something as foolhardy as to fall in love with Daisy. He couldn't. Not with the guilt he carries over his past sins… Not when he has no right to her heart…But perhaps, just perhaps, she can forgive the past and trust that he'd forever cherish her heart—but will she let him?

The Love of a Rogue
Book 3 in the "Heart of a Duke" Series

Lady Imogen Moore hasn't had an easy time of it since she made her Come Out. With her betrothed, a powerful duke breaking it off to wed her sister, she's become the *tons* favorite piece of gossip. Never again wanting to experience the pain of a broken heart, she's resolved to make a match with a polite, respectable gentleman. The last thing she wants is another reckless rogue.

Lord Alex Edgerton has a problem. His brother, tired of Alex's carousing has charged him with chaperoning their remaining, unwed sister about *ton* events. Shopping? No, thank you. Attending the theatre? He'd rather be at Forbidden Pleasures with a scantily clad beauty upon his lap. The task of *chaperone* becomes even more of a bother when his sister drags along her dearest friend, Lady Imogen to social functions. The last thing he wants in his life is a young, innocent English miss.

Except, as Alex and Imogen are thrown together, passions flare and Alex comes to find he not only wants Imogen in his bed, but also in his heart. Yet now he must convince Imogen to risk all, on the heart of a rogue.

More Than a Duke
Book 2 in the "Heart of a Duke" Series

Polite Society doesn't take Lady Anne Adamson seriously. However, Anne isn't just another pretty young miss. When she discovers her father betrayed her mother's love and her family descended into poverty, Anne comes up with a plan to marry a respectable, powerful, and honorable gentleman—a man nothing like her philandering father.

Armed with the heart of a duke pendant, fabled to land the wearer a duke's heart, she decides to enlist the aid of the notorious Harry, 6th Earl of Stanhope. A scoundrel with a scandalous past, he is the last gentleman she'd ever wed...however, his reputation marks him the perfect man to school her in the art of seduction so she might ensnare the illustrious Duke of Crawford.

Harry, the Earl of Stanhope is a jaded, cynical rogue who lives for his own pleasures. Having been thrown over by the only woman he ever loved so she could wed a duke, he's not at all surprised when Lady Anne approaches him with her scheme to capture another duke's affection. He's come to appreciate that all women are in fact greedy, title-grasping, self-indulgent creatures. And with Anne's history of grating on his every last nerve, she is the last woman he'd ever agree to school in the art of seduction. Only his friendship with the lady's sister compels him to help.

What begins as a pretend courtship, born of lessons on seduction, becomes something more leaving Anne to decide if she can give her heart to a reckless rogue, and Harry must decide if he's willing to again trust in a lady's love.

For Love of the Duke
Book 1 in the "Heart of a Duke" Series

After the tragic death of his wife, Jasper, the 8th Duke of Bainbridge buried himself away in the dark cold walls of his home, Castle Blackwood. When he's coaxed out of his self-imposed exile to attend the amusements of the Frost Fair, his life is irrevocably changed by his fateful meeting with Lady Katherine Adamson.

With her tight brown ringlets and silly white-ruffled gowns, Lady Katherine Adamson has found her dance card empty for two Seasons. After her father's passing, Katherine learned the unreliability of men, and is determined to depend on no one, except herself. Until she meets Jasper…

In a desperate bid to avoid a match arranged by her family, Katherine makes the Duke of Bainbridge a shocking proposition—one that he accepts.

Only, as Katherine begins to love Jasper, she finds the arrangement agreed upon is not enough. And Jasper is left to decide if protecting his heart is more important than fighting for Katherine's love.

In Need of a Duke
A Prequel Novella to "The Heart of a Duke" Series

In Need of a Duke: (Author's Note: This is a prequel novella to "The Heart of a Duke" series by Christi Caldwell. It was originally available in "The Heart of a Duke" Collection and is now being published as an individual novella.

It features a new prologue and epilogue.

Years earlier, a gypsy woman passed to Lady Aldora Adamson and her friends a heart pendant that promised them each the heart of a duke.

Now, a young lady, with her family facing ruin and scandal, Lady Aldora doesn't have time for mythical stories about cheap baubles. She needs to save her sisters and brother by marrying a titled gentleman with wealth and power to his name. She sets her bespectacled sights upon the Marquess of St. James.

Turned out by his father after a tragic scandal, Lord Michael Knightly has grown into a powerful, but self-made man. With the whispers and stares that still follow him, he would rather be anywhere but London…

Until he meets Lady Aldora, a young woman who mistakes him for his brother, the Marquess of St. James. The connection between Aldora and Michael is immediate and as they come to know one another, Aldora's feelings for Michael war with her sisterly responsibilities. With her family's dire situation, a man of Michael's scandalous past will never do.

Ultimately, Aldora must choose between her responsibilities as a sister and her love for Michael.

BIOGRAPHY

Christi Caldwell is the *USA Today* bestselling author of the Sinful Brides series and the Heart of a Duke series. She blames novelist Judith McNaught for luring her into the world of historical romance. When Christi was at the University of Connecticut, she began writing her own tales of love—ones where even the most perfect heroes and heroines had imperfections. She learned to enjoy torturing her couples before they earned their well-deserved happily ever after. Christi lives in North Carolina where she spends her time writing, baking, and being a mommy to the most inspiring little boy and empathetic, spirited girls who, with their mischievous twin antics, offer an endless source of story ideas!

Visit www.christicaldwellauthor.com to learn more about what Christi is working on, or join her on Facebook at Christi Caldwell Author, and Twitter @ChristiCaldwell!

Printed in Great Britain
by Amazon